Suddenly there was a flash of scarlet

Evelina threw up an arm to shade her eyes. "A redbird. He's beautiful."

"We have a saying in these parts," Ryan drawled. "See a redbird before sunset, and you'll be kissed before nightfall."

"That's hardly likely."

His grin was maddeningly inviting. "You're with a villain, remember? I might take advantage of you."

Another two hundred yards and they'd be at the house. She moved forward.

"Hold on a minute," he said, and she stopped.

He closed the gap between them, but she stepped back, opening it again. He took another step, and so did she, which left her wedged against a tree. She wasn't going anywhere and she knew it. There was barely an inch between them now. He pressed forward anyway, and then he kissed her....

Dear Reader,

Old cowboy movies unraveled for us exciting tales of two-fisted, rugged heroes who could handle everything from range wars to cattle stampedes without losing their cool or their Stetsons. We were told long and often that our strong, silent cowboy was earthy and honest. He had no patience for frippery and pretense. He loved his horse. He loved the tangy smell of sagebrush, the high blue skies and the wide-open spaces.

In our hearts we knew that such a man would have deep, unharnessed emotions as well. But these tales only hinted at how he loved and needed the woman in his life. We were told that in the West, men were men. But we were never shown.

Maybe this lack is why, over the years, fewer and fewer Western movies were made. We no longer have the patience to fill in the gaps. Maybe, too, this is why there has been such a big swing to country music, where deep feelings are set out in the open.

Today we don't want to read between the lines. We want stories that tell us what we knew all along. That what drove the hard-muscled and sometimes hardheaded man of yesterday is the same thing that drives him today and will drive him tomorrow— love for that special woman who makes everything worthwhile.

Now, thanks to Harlequin, we can go Back to the Ranch and thrill to the real story. The whole story.

Sincerely,

Virginia Hart

THE PERFECT SCOUNDREL
Virginia Hart

Harlequin Books

TORONTO • NEW YORK • LONDON
AMSTERDAM • PARIS • SYDNEY • HAMBURG
STOCKHOLM • ATHENS • TOKYO • MILAN
MADRID • WARSAW • BUDAPEST • AUCKLAND

ISBN 0-373-03305-2

THE PERFECT SCOUNDREL

CHAPTER ONE

"FILL IT WITH REGULAR, please," Evelina told the jean-clad man who sauntered out of the service station. "And would you check under the hood?"

Tall and lazy-looking, his expression rather high-and-mighty, he stopped to lean one hand against the soft-drink machine and contemplate the selections. Singing along with the tinny-sounding radio that was belting out something about honky-tonk dreams, he obviously considered his choice of beverage more important than her business.

The garb of employees in small-town gas stations was clearly more informal than it was in the city. Still, worn blue denims, ragged at the knees, and a white shirt with the sleeves rolled up, rather than a spiffy coverall with a name embroidered on the pocket? Badly scuffed cowboy boots?

Maybe his pose, one that emphasized muscles a weight lifter wouldn't scorn, was meant to impress her. He could have saved the effort. Conan the Barbarian couldn't have unsettled her in this heat.

Ouch! The something she thought she'd gotten out of her eye twenty minutes earlier, was still there, stinging and blurring her vision. The air-conditioning didn't work, and she'd been forced to drive with the windows open to enable herself to breathe. So what could she expect?

Although her nut-brown hair had been gathered into a convenient knot atop her head when she'd left home, it hadn't stayed there. Windblown now, it no doubt resembled a nest constructed by a nearsighted squirrel. Not only that, she'd chewed off all her lipstick.

No rest-room sign on the left side of the building. None on the right. Super.

So far, the service-station attendant wasn't attending to anything. At least, he wasn't attending to her car, nor the dusty green pickup in the next aisle.

"Are the rest rooms inside?" she asked. Her throat was dry, making her sound like the Wicked Witch of the East—or was it the West? No matter. He didn't deserve any better.

Too busy adding his own harmony to the radio song to bother with an answer, he only nodded. He punched one of the plastic squares on the machine, waited for the ka-thunk and reached into the chute.

"Thank you," she said, trying not to let his attitude bother her.

She knew how he felt. It was even hotter here in Fortune, Texas—population 3,567, according to the town's Welcome sign—than it had been in Houston. After a swig of his iced pop and a final note of twangy harmony, she imagined he'd be flying around her car as his more neatly uniformed counterparts in TV commercials did, thrusting the gasoline nozzle into the tank with one hand, checking the inflation of her tires with the other and shining her windshield as he whistled.

Darn. The rest-room door was locked. He might have told her. She went back out.

"May I have the key?" she asked.

"On the wall inside to your right. Help yourself." He gestured with his root beer.

"Thank you," she said, weighting the two syllables with all the sarcasm they could hold this time. She had, after all, not brought the heat with her. Nor had she chosen his line of work for him.

The rest room was sparkling clean and air-conditioned, more than making up for the attendant's failure to snap to attention. After treating her face to a dozen delicious splashes of cool water, her parched lips to a fresh application of Spiced Peach lip gloss and her windblown locks to a combing and repinning that restored their resemblance to hair, she tucked her wilted yellow cotton shirt into the waistband of her rumpled white chinos.

There. She would have to do.

Her eye felt better, too. She must have flushed out the speck of dust while she was washing. Now for an orange soda, if she was in luck and the machine stocked them. Otherwise, she'd have a . . .

Unbelievably, the attendant was still working on his drink. Could he have already filled her tank? No. And she could see that the windshield was still spotted with unfortunate insects.

"Sir? My car?"

"You're at the self-service pump," he drawled, not moving.

"I . . ." Her gaze swing to the carefully printed sign that told her he was right. "Oh, so I am."

Before she could ask sweetly if it would have broken his back to fill the tank, anyway, she again felt a sharp jab of pain in her eye, forcing it closed. "Darn!"

"Got something in your eye?"

Wasn't it obvious? "A speck of road dust. I was driving with the windows down and—"

"Let's have a look." He lumbered toward her.

"No!" Holding a protective hand over the injured eye, she backed away, determined not to allow those huge square hands, probably as dexterous as boxing gloves, to make the damage worse.

"I don't think you should. But thank you. I'll just go into the washroom again and—"

"Hold still." Grasping her shoulders firmly, he forced her backward until the rim of a metal trash can against the wall dug into the backs of her knees.

"Please," she protested, squirming ineffectively.

"Easy does it." He leaned close, thrusting out a generous lower lip as he apparently considered what procedure to follow.

"The eye is an extremely delicate—"

"Keep still."

"But—"

"Your mouth," he cut in. "Keep it still, too." So close now she could see herself in the depths of his almost ebony eyes and smell the masculine scent of his skin, he squinted at her as if she were something under a microscope. Holding her firmly in place, he reached into his back pocket and brought out a handkerchief. He made a point of one corner and dabbed at the smarting orb so lightly she hardly felt it.

Curling her toes into her sandals, she stifled an outcry with effort.

"No speck." His chocolate-brown mustache twitched with the triumphant announcement.

"I know when I have something in my eye."

"It was an eyelash." He held up the offending bit, still attached to the point of the handkerchief, as though he thought she might want to bronze it to commemorate the occasion.

"Thank you very much for your help," she said tightly.

"Anytime." He touched his fingers to his forehead in the kind of salute that would have gone well with a ten-gallon hat and a pair of six guns.

Opening and closing her eyes several times, she looked from one side to the other, expecting the pain to strike again. It didn't. By some miracle, his operation had been a success.

After that, how could she berate him for being such a clod about her car? Giving her ignition keys an impatient shake, she started toward it. She felt like a schoolgirl caught by the vice-principal going up the down staircase and having to go back and start over.

"I'll move my car to the full-service island," she announced.

"Good idea."

Grr. "Any preference as to which pump I use?"

"Suit yourself." Three long strides carried him to the mechanic's area, where he leaned in and shouted. "Hey, Harry. You've got a customer."

"Harry?" Evelina's hand fell away from the car door. "Don't *you* work here?"

"Nope." Mischief gleamed in the dark eyes again and he almost smiled. "I just came in for a fill-up."

"Oh." Without further comment, she watched as he climbed into the dusty green pickup, backed within inches of a gas pump and screeched forward again to the exit.

"Take it easy," he said, favoring her with another cowboy-style salute.

It wasn't until he was out of sight that it struck her. What had she been thinking of? How had she allowed him to get away? He was perfect. Exactly what she was looking for!

A balding man with the name Harry embroidered in red on the pocket of his baggy gray coverall shuffled toward her, wiping his hands on a rag. "How do, little lady. Fill 'er up?"

"Yes. No. I mean, later." Evelina looked in the direction the pickup had gone. The gallon or so she had left in the tank would have to be enough. She couldn't afford any delay.

CHAPTER TWO

HE DIDN'T HAVE much of a head start. Surely she could catch up to him. On the other hand, cruising speed would have taken him from one end of Main Street to the other in two minutes. Once on the highway, he could have pushed the accelerator to the floor.

It was also possible he was an out-of-towner only passing through. No. He'd called the service-station man by name and he'd had the self-assurance of someone firmly planted on his own turf.

Wait. She did a double take and slowed. The green pickup was parked at the curb on her right in the middle of the block. Now, was he in Calvin's Café, the Sundown Real Estate office or the Swiss Miss Bakery?

Her first guess was correct. Besides the man behind the counter and a pretty, red-haired waitress in green-and-white checkered apron and cap, only three other people were in the café—an elderly couple in one of the booths, and the man Evelina had been pursuing at the counter.

"May I sit here?" she asked, raising her voice to be heard over the whir of two standing fans that were doing a heroic job of cooling the narrow, L-shaped room.

"Help yourself," he said.

If he was puzzled by her arrival, he didn't show it. Maybe—probably—he was accustomed to being followed by females. Now that she was looking at him with two good eyes, no longer judging him by what she'd assumed was a slipshod attention to his job, she could see that he was handsome and very sexy. She didn't usually care for mustaches, but on this man it was almost appealing. He had a wide forehead, crisply curling dark brown hair, a strong straight nose and well-defined cheekbones.

She glanced at his left hand. No wedding ring. But he might have been one of those holdouts who thought only the female of the species should be tagged as "taken."

Seemingly unaware of her appraisal, he accepted the hot dog the counterman put in front of him and began to douse it beyond recognition with catsup. Suddenly he turned and asked her solicitously, "Would you like something? A cold beer? A hot dog? A bowl of chili?"

"Nothing, thanks." She twisted her stool toward him and prepared to make her speech. "I don't mean to intrude. But I was so excited when I saw you back there, I couldn't wait to get to you. You're exactly the man I've been looking for."

His expression didn't change. He didn't so much as lift an eyebrow. But the counterman emitted a snort that might have become a laugh, if he hadn't stifled it with his hand. "Anything else for you today, Ryan?" he asked.

"A tall buttermilk with a side of chipped ice, and that'll do it, Calvin."

"Sure thing."

Buttermilk with a hot dog? Evelina tried not to wrinkle her nose in distaste at the prospect of the odious combination. And that on top of the root beer he'd downed at the gas station?

"Your name's Ryan?" she asked pleasantly, hoping he'd tell her if it was a first or last name so she could use it correctly. When he didn't, she went on, "I'm Evelina Pettit."

She hesitated, wanting to polish her words before saying them. Odd. She'd said the same words, or words very much like them, to countless other people, ever since the day she'd volunteered to teach classes at a community center in Houston.

Usually it was as if she were equipped with a push button that would release the message without any conscious thought on her part. This time the built-in program didn't seem to be in proper working order. Whether it was the heat of the day, the fact that she hadn't had much sleep the night before or the distraction of the remarkable deep brown eyes, like no other eyes she'd ever seen, that had her confused, she wasn't certain.

"Are . . . are you free tonight?" she managed.

The mustache twitched. Did it cover a smile or a sneer? "What did you have in mind?"

She patted the back of her hair where one of the pins was working free again. She knew that her face, damp from the ovenlike heat and from the rush she'd been in to follow him, would be shiny. Her mascara might even be smudged under her eyes, waterproof claims to the contrary. It was difficult to remain businesslike when she couldn't help wondering if she looked like Alice Cooper.

"Actually I'm interested in more than just tonight," she said, injecting self-possession into her voice.

The counterman snorted again, pretended to cough and busied himself polishing the already-gleaming sugar dispenser.

"I'm Evelina Pettit from Houston," she began again, fascinated by the unique way this Ryan poured buttermilk over the chipped ice before downing it, without getting any of it on his mustache in the process.

"Evelina," he repeated, interest narrowing his eyes beneath his shaggy, inverted-V brows.

"I can't tell you how surprised I am to find the man I want so quickly. I'd expected to have to meet and talk to a dozen or more before I could come to a decision."

"Is that right?" He exchanged glances with the counterman, then stood up and took Evelina's elbow, steering her to one of the booths. "I think we'll be more comfortable over here."

"Fine." It didn't matter where they sat. She only wanted to say what she had to say and get on with business. "I represent the..." she began, when she'd been tucked into place.

But Ryan had gone back to get his sandwich and buttermilk. She waited until he was settled across from her before she began again. Now it was worse than ever. With the blinds closed against the sun, the corner was dim. The elderly couple had paid their bill and left, and there was something uncomfortably intimate about the way this man, Ryan, was looking at her.

Then it struck her. It was just as well that she *had* been interrupted. With this particular project, she wasn't representing anyone but herself, and her younger sister, Faye, of course.

"I think I will have something to drink," she said, raising a hand to signal the man behind the counter. "Do you have iced tea?" she asked him.

"Like the sign says. Small or large?"

"Large," Ryan answered for her.

"Let me give you my card." She dug into her flat, no-nonsense purse, plucked out a business card and waited while he read it.

He groaned and handed it back to her. "Hell, I knew this was too good to be true." He leaned against the back of the plastic-upholstered booth.

"What?"

"A pretty girl coming up to me, telling me I'm exactly what she's looking for." He shook his head.

Her hazel eyes widened and she swallowed. "I hope, uh, you didn't think..."

"I guess I didn't. Not really. Anyway, I get the picture now. You've singled me out for one free lesson at this dancing school of yours. The catch is I have to sign up for a five-thousand-dollar course to get it. You'll guarantee I learn to dance the fox-trot, the waltz, the chicken, the horned toad or whatever they're calling the latest steps this year." He wadded up his napkin, dropped it on his plate and started to get up. "Sorry. I decline."

"Wait." She caught his arm and pulled him back. "It's nothing like that. Hear me out."

He pressed his lips together briefly. "You've got five minutes. Do you get points if you can convince someone to listen?"

"Want lemon with this tea?" the counterman asked, putting the glass in front of her.

"No, thank you." She tore the paper off her straw, plunged it into her drink and took a healthy sip. "Plans are in the works for a Return to Good Fortune celebration. I suppose you've heard of it."

"I've heard. But nobody much cottoned to the idea, as I recall." His eyes narrowed. "You're not a dance teacher?"

"No. That is, yes. I'm a teacher at Garfield High School in Houston. But that has nothing to do with what I'm talking about." She fluttered one hand, wanting to still his questions until she had finished. "As you probably know, when this town was settled, it was called Good Fortune, because of a boom in oil and the resulting prosperity."

He nodded, apparently willing to humor her. "Right."

"Over the years, most of the wells played out, and the 'Good' was dropped."

"So?"

"So our idea is to put the 'Good' back again—at least for one weekend in early August. Everybody will dress in old-fashioned costumes. There'll be square dancing, bonfires, games and contests. And to start it off, a musical show based on high points in the town's history."

"A musical show. You must know Kurt Warren's wife." He crossed his arms over his chest and leaned back again. "She's new in town. And the way I understand, she got bored with wide open spaces and decided to drag the big city out here."

"It wasn't like that."

"If you know the lady, you know she didn't get very far with the idea. It got so folks ducked into doorways when they saw her coming."

"Faye Warren is my sister," Evelina said tightly.

"Sisters." Ryan studied her for a long moment as if trying to discern a likeness. "So she sent for reinforcements."

"It's a big job for one person."

"An *impossible* job would describe it better." He hooted. "You actually think you'll get support for this kind of show here?"

"I don't think. I *know*." Evelina frowned. His lack of enthusiasm for the Return to Good Fortune weekend sobered her. According to Faye's letters, when she'd approached people with her proposed celebration, they'd stumbled over each other to take part. Maybe Ryan was one of those ranchers who spent so much time on the range he seldom got into civilization. "You must have an auditorium somewhere in town. A building with a stage."

"The movie theater is usually available," Ryan said. "At a price. Or the high school gymnasium. But how will you get your audience? At gunpoint?"

Ignoring his sarcasm, she leaned forward on her elbows.

"That's where *you* come in."

"Me?" He jabbed a thumb at his chest. "Do I look like the strong-arm type?"

"Of course not."

"As your sister found out, most folks here don't punch time clocks and they don't quit at five. They work a long hard day and want to relax when they get the chance. Nobody I know'll sit through a play put on by outsiders, and I don't have the magic wand it would take to drag them into a theater, air-conditioned or not."

"It won't take a magic wand, I assure you."

"Care to bet on that?"

It wasn't true that his eyes were like no other eyes she'd ever known. They were very much like Kurt's eyes. Oh, they were a darker, more mysterious shade of brown, and they were deeper set, but they had the same sparkle, the same way of appearing to laugh all the time, so that it was difficult to know when he was serious.

Kurt's eyes had laughed at her the day he broke the news that he was in love with someone else. No. Not just someone else. He was in love with her sister. In her heart of hearts Evelina had known it for weeks. She'd even anticipated it before Faye came home from college and the two met. It was inevitable. Every man who met Faye fell madly in love with her.

"You may think this is a place," Ryan was saying, "where we sit and watch the grass grow. Where we get all aflutter at the prospect of a dancing show put on by city folk. T'aint so, Evvie. We have TV. Daytime soaps and nighttime soaps. We have '60 Minutes' and 'Cheers' reruns. Just like in Houston." He turned his wrist and squinted at his watch. A huge ugly thing with a yellowed face and a thick leather band. "Gotta run now. Nice talking to you. And I wish you luck. You're gonna need it."

"You promised me five minutes."

"Five, ten minutes—an hour won't help. Sorry."

"Sit down." She slapped a hand on the table, too irritated by his attitude to manage a smile. "I have at least two minutes left."

He registered surprise at her vehement reaction, but remained standing. "You've got the floor."

"What if I can convince you that people will not only attend the show, they'll flock to the box office in droves? That it'll be a sellout?"

"What odds you giving?" Calvin asked, out of the corner of his mouth, no longer attempting to disguise the fact that he was listening.

Evelina ignored him. "What if I can further convince you that they'll pay ten dollars apiece for the privilege of filling the auditorium?"

"You're a witch, right?" Ryan allowed his bitter-sweet eyes to ride over her for effect. "Do you wiggle your nose? Or just your hips?"

"That isn't funny, Ryan," the waitress broke in, coming over to join the debate. "She's only trying to do her job. Besides, you aren't giving her a very good idea of Fortune hospitality."

Ryan swiveled around to look at her. "Would you attend this extravaganza, Noreen?"

The woman adjusted the ties of her apron and gave her short curly hairdo a pat. "Well...I don't know. I've got the kids to look after when I get home from work and—"

"Would you?"

She sighed. "Not me, maybe. I'm not one of your night people."

When Ryan turned back to Evelina, he wore a smug expression. "Is that plain enough for you?"

"What if I tell you that after expenses, the money we take in will go back to the town? For whatever your town council decides it needs. A recreation center. Landscaping for the park—"

"A statue of our most prominent citizen for the public square?" His grin was maddeningly attractive, she had to admit, even though it was aimed derisively at her. He was likely a big fish in this small pond, which was why he stayed here, rather than taking his dubious charm to the city. He would lean, no doubt, toward leggy blondes, who squealed when they felt his muscles and favored him with you-great-big-wonderful-man glances. Certainly he felt she should be honored just to be sitting across from him. Might make her whole futile trip worthwhile.

"If a statue is what you want," she answered.

One shaggy eyebrow lifted and the other lowered. He was one of those people who gave away very little of what he was thinking—and what he was thinking was anybody's guess, though she would have bet it wasn't very flattering.

"Folks here are as charitable as folks anywhere else," he began, as if explaining the facts of life to a not-too-bright child. "They give their all when the need arises, but they want value for value."

"They'll get value. Not only will they be giving to a worthy cause, they'll be receiving entertainment."

He grinned more widely. "There's a mighty big question mark after the word 'entertainment.'"

Grr. He was impossible.

How she longed to tell him what she thought of him. But she didn't dare. Even if she couldn't convince him to cooperate with her plan, she didn't want him as an enemy. He might be in a position to make things difficult for her here.

"Terlinga has its Chili Cook-Off," she went on. "New Braunfels has its Sausage Festival. San Marcos has its canoe races. Huntsville, its Texas Prison Rodeo. On and on."

"And the point is...?"

"With a little work, this celebration could put Fortune on the map. It could bring back some of the tourist money it lost when the highway was rerouted."

Apparently unimpressed, Ryan called to Calvin, "Want to fix me another of those hot dogs to go?"

"Sure thing. Want to get that order, Noreen?" Busy filling a paper-napkin dispenser, Calvin peered over the top of his steel-rimmed glasses at the waitress, who'd been sitting at a nearby table listening to the exchange.

"That is, if you think you've had enough of a coffee break. Wouldn't want to overwork you."

"Guess it'll have to do, boss."

She scribbled something on her order pad, and hooked it over the edge of her apron pocket. Then she turned to Evelina. "Fortune never was on the map, honey, even before the highway. Most of us like it that way, you know? Your sister was fighting a losing battle. Besides, we don't have much history to sing about. Nothing noteworthy ever happened here."

"Except the time the Hardcastle boy came back from Oklahoma City with a monkey for a pet," Calvin drawled.

"You remember that?" Noreen laughed. "And the night it opened its cage and escaped?"

"How could I forget?" Calvin's shoulders shook with his creaky laugh. "Here he was, yanking clothes off all the clotheslines, then running through the beauty parlor. All those ladies sitting under the driers, screaming."

"Then the little beast scrambled up the old oak in the town square and dropped acorns on the men when they tried to coax him down." Noreen shook her head. "It was real funny. But it wouldn't add up to enough to make up a play."

"Every town has a history," Evelina insisted. "It might surprise you. Fortune had its share of problems with cattlemen versus sheep men, with marauding outlaws and with the arrival of the barbed-wire fence. That's the beauty of it. The story could be about Anytown, Texas, and its beginnings. It'll draw people from all over the state if there's enough publicity."

"Will Clint Eastwood be in the cast? Sylvester Stallone?" Ryan held up one hand, not waiting for her reply. "Then you haven't convinced me."

Evelina sighed. "Sorry about that."

"We could still get together tonight, though," he said.

How kind of him to offer himself as consolation prize! "I believe I'll decline, regretfully."

"There's a place just outside of town that has catfish to make your trip here worthwhile. Not to mention homemade pie better'n your momma makes."

"I don't care for catfish. And my mother's a lousy cook."

"You'll like this catfish. And the cook's great."

She hesitated. Her sense of good business told her to accept. Maybe between salad and coffee she could convince him to take part in her project. Or was she only rationalizing? Would she truly be sacrificing her time to the cause? Or would she be going out with him because he was wickedly attractive and she was stirred by him in spite of herself?

No. She wasn't planning to earn a cameo spot in his little black book. A book where women he dated were probably graded A, B or C, according to his interest in them.

"We have excellent restaurants in Houston," she said, more snap in her voice than she'd intended.

"I know. I've been there a time or two. But you don't have any like this one."

"Who does the acting in the play, honey?" Noreen asked, plunking a brown paper bag on the counter.

"That's where the fun comes in," Evelina answered, grateful that *someone* was courteous enough to give her a hearing. "Except for a few key people we bring in from a professional troupe we've worked with before, all parts will be played by local people." She fastened Ryan with a smug look. "Experience has taught me that people are people, wherever they live. However thrifty they are with their hard-earned dollars, they *do* attend a show if their friends and neighbors are in it."

"Maybe it isn't such a bad idea." Ryan picked up his bag. "Folks likely *will* pay to see other folks make fools of themselves. And that's where I came in, right? You're a talent scout."

"You could say that."

"You wanted me for a part in this play?"

So even *his* thick skull had allowed an idea to penetrate.

"That's right."

A smile played on his lips. "I'm flattered."

"You should be," she went on, feeling the glow of victory. She'd managed to nudge his ego. "I don't just want you for one of the parts. I want you for the most important part."

"The leading man?"

"No. For Blackjack Sykes, the leader of the outlaw band who's helping the ruthless cattle baron snatch up the small ranches whatever the cost. You'd be perfect. Your mustache gives just the right touch, and that wicked gleam in your eye is exactly what we'll need when you order your men to torch the ranches if the folks haven't cleared out by sundown."

Calvin guffawed. "The lady's got your number, Ryan."

Ryan colored slightly. "I hate to disappoint you, Evvie. But my schedule doesn't permit that much time off."

Evvie. That was the second time he'd called her that. How she hated the diminutive. "You're a rancher, aren't you?"

He nodded.

"Spring roundup is over," she said. Faye had told her that much. After weeks of rattling around the house by herself while Kurt was out playing cowboy, her sister actually got to see him once in a while now. "You have time on your hands."

"You think roundup is all there is to ranching?"

"Isn't it, basically?"

"We're even." He chuckled. "You know as much about ranching as I do about singing and dancing."

"I've read books on the subject," she said, not ready to give up on him yet. "I discovered, for instance, that cowboys of the Old West actually did sing to their horses." Which maybe explained the not-bad-at-all singing voice she'd heard him display earlier.

"They still do. The sound gentles the animals. Keeps 'em from getting spooked at sudden noises."

"That makes sense."

"Well—" he gestured with his take-out bag "—be seeing you around, Evvie. I hope. And again, good luck."

When he started for the door this time, she could tell he meant business. There was little chance of getting him to sit down and reconsider. "You'd have a total of twenty lines," she called after him. "Short ones. And two little songs."

He stopped and turned back to face her. "You expect me to climb up on the stage and sing?"

"What else? It's a musical. But you don't have to worry. Your friends won't expect Pavarotti."

Ryan's only comment was a grunt.

"I heard you singing today," she reminded him. "At the station."

The gleam was back in his eyes. "Would you want it with or without guitar?"

"With, preferably. But it wouldn't be necessary." She clasped her hands together, hoping that gleam meant he was weakening. "Besides that, you'd only draw your gun a time or two, twitch your mustache and look hateful. That shouldn't be too hard for you."

"Thanks a heap."

"I didn't mean that the way it sounded."

He studied her a long moment. "Why the heavy? Why aren't you offering me the hero part?"

She caught her lower lip between her teeth. So it *was* an ego problem. He saw himself as the golden defender of womankind. "If we want to get it orchestrated in time, the hero, by necessity, will have to be a member of the professional Houston-based troupe I mentioned. His is a large part and requires dancing, as well as singing. Maybe by next year though . . ."

"Next year?" Ryan looked astonished.

"Why not? It might be so much fun people will want to keep it as an annual event. Anyway, it wouldn't do for the leading man to have a mustache."

"Leading men don't have mustaches?"

"Heroes have to look wholesome."

"Yep," Calvin muttered. "That sure lets you out."

"Sorry, but no way I'm gonna play nasty old Sykes." Again Ryan started away and again he stopped, this time with a hand gripping the doorknob. "Sure you won't change your mind about that catfish?"

"Sure you won't change your mind about the part?"

He shook his head slowly. "I guess what we've got here is a standoff."

"I guess we have."

It was too bad, she mused, as she watched him climb into his truck and roar off. She usually chose her performers by instinct, and she'd been so certain this time that her instincts were correct.

She got to her feet and walked over to the counter. "Is there a farmhouse close to town where the owner might allow us to rehearse and to park the van the night of the performance?" she asked Calvin, deciding not to dwell on the negative. "I'd pay something, and guarantee there'd be no problems."

Noreen began to wipe the tabletop in the booth where Ryan and Evelina had been sitting. "Our place is too small," she said, "or I'd be glad to help."

"Hell, Noreen," Calvin snorted, "your old man would chase you with a broom if you brought in a bunch of outsiders. He likes his TV in peace at night."

"That's true." The waitress tilted her head to one side, thinking.

"Hold on." Calvin snapped his fingers. "How about Amy Garrison?"

"I don't think so," Noreen said, her mouth pulling down at the corners.

"Why not? Amy's good-natured and friendly."

"Yeah. But it's not a good idea, and you know it."

"She's got lots of room. There's that big old barn, and she loves company. The more the merrier."

"Where is Mrs. Garrison's house?" Evelina asked quickly, wanting to get the information before Noreen talked him out of the idea.

If there were problems with the Garrison woman, she was confident she could iron them out. Most people, she'd discovered, could find use for the extra money she was offering. Even in some of the big ranches, she'd heard, people often had trouble with cash flow.

Calvin scratched his head. "Head out the highway, oh, about two miles. Till you see a long stretch of white fence on your left and a lot of horses. A hundred yards or so along, a road'll come in on your right. Follow it till you see this big yellow house sitting way back all by itself. There's a swinging sign over the drive that says Tully T Ranch."

"Tully T. I don't see how I can miss it. Thank you. I'll give it a try."

"Oh, Miss Pettit . . ." The man followed her to the door.

"Yes?"

"Think you could use a banjo picker in this theatrical of yours? I'm mighty handy with one, if I do say so myself."

"I don't know why not," she said, trying not to giggle as she allowed the screen door to slap behind her.

Bustling metropolis or one-horse town. People were basically the same. Everybody wanted to be in show business.

CHAPTER THREE

AN INVITING SHADE of yellow, with neat white trim and a wraparound porch, the Garrison house sat some distance from the road. Its gravel driveway, bordered with a riot of summer flowers, made a gentle arc between the well-kept outbuildings and corrals.

The woman who came to meet the car was tall and big-boned with neatly cropped silver-gray hair and a wide smile. She'd been weeding, she said, and welcomed an excuse to stop. She introduced herself as Amy Garrison and ushered Evelina inside.

"I think it's a lovely idea," Amy said, after listening with interest to the plans for a Return to Good Fortune celebration. "Bless Calvin for suggesting me."

Evelina blessed Calvin, too. Finding such a welcome almost made up for losing the villain of her choice. Why had Noreen questioned the wisdom of using Amy? The woman was indeed good-natured and friendly.

"There's been talk of a historical pageant," Amy went on. "Kurt Warren's bride tried to get support for it. To no avail, I'm afraid. Do you know her?"

"She's my sister."

"Oh?" Amy didn't question the lack of resemblance between the sisters, as most people did when the relationship was revealed. But her eyes held the puzzled look Evelina often saw.

"Then you're working on the Good Fortune Weekend together."

"Yes. My sister ran into a few snags and asked me to come and help."

Amy nodded. "My neighbors haven't been very cooperative. Some are slow to accept new ideas."

So Ryan had been telling the truth.

"I'm beginning to find that out." Feeling comfortable with Amy at once, Evelina told her about the run-in she'd had at the service station and again at the café with the swelled head who'd pooh-poohed her plans.

"Maybe he was shy," Amy suggested.

"That one, shy? Hah! More likely he expected to be treated as if he'd just stepped down from Valhalla."

"Conceited?"

"You know the type. You should have seen him swagger." Evelina pressed the back of her hand to her forehead for emphasis. "It's too bad. He's a casting director's dream."

Had he truly swaggered? Or was she only wanting to talk about him? To be fair, he'd walked with an animal grace that could have come naturally. The image of him loomed before her again, making her recall details that hadn't registered in her conscious mind at the time.

She saw him walking toward her, his head cocked to one side, his wide shoulders moving with his stride, his sinewy arms swinging slightly, the lines of his lower body defined clearly in form-fitting jeans.

And she saw him walking away. His—

Enough!

She blinked to chase away the thoughts taking form in her weary brain and concentrated on his face. It was a thought-provoking face admittedly. And he had dimples. No. Not dimples. Just one. In his left cheek. One of his eyebrows raised higher than the other when he was conveying skepticism, and his smile was the slow-spreading sort that began with a mere twitch of his sculpted lips.

An asymmetrical face, she realized now that she thought about it. Why had it snagged in her memory, disturbing her? Making her want to prove to him how wrong he'd been? Making her want to put on such a terrific show the whole town would be talking about it for weeks? Worse, making her feel warm and at the same time chilled, as if a thousand ants with icy feet were skittering up and down her backbone?

"The perfect scoundrel, eh?" Amy said in amusement. "Don't fret. This town is teeming with cads. We'll ferret one out to suit you."

It was a pleasant old house. The floors were polished parquet, covered with hooked rugs in brilliant floral patterns. The furniture was antique and appeared to have been selected lovingly piece by piece. Nothing matched, but the total effect was charming. A player piano took the place of honor, and perhaps in deference to summer, the fieldstone fireplace had been set about with a tangle of enthusiastic potted plants.

Evelina hadn't been there fifteen minutes before she'd accepted not only an invitation for dinner, but one for breakfast. Faye wasn't expecting her until the next morning, anyway. Amy wouldn't hear of her staying in the stuffy hotel in town, whose lobby was filled with "old duffers watching the ball game." Besides, the time together would allow her a chance to suggest some fellow townspeople who might be willing to fill out the cast.

"For instance, I have the perfect candidate for your pitiful little old widow."

"Who?"

"Me. I have an outdated, too-long dress that made me look like Whistler's mother when it was new. If I throw a moth-eaten dresser scarf around my shoulders for a shawl, you'd be surprised how pathetic I can look. There won't be a dry eye in the house when the rustlers threaten to burn me out."

"You?" Before Evelina could give voice to the obvious discrepancy between Amy's robust appearance and the shivering browbeaten woman in the play, tires crunched on the gravel driveway and the woman flew to the window.

"My son was picking up some ice cream when he was in town," she said. "Twenty-five flavors at the drugstore, and what do you bet he brings home vanilla?"

Footsteps sounded on the porch, the screen door slapped, and the perfect scoundrel sauntered in. Taking a pose reminiscent of the one that had irritated Evelina at the service station, Ryan raised one eyebrow and fixed his bold gaze on her.

She stood up and her purse flopped to the floor. She retrieved it, set it too close to the edge of the coffee table and it fell again. She left it.

Amy couldn't possibly have missed the crackle of antagonism in the air. "You two know each other?"

Ryan fluttered an accusing hand in Evelina's direction.

"She tried to sweet-talk me into making a jackass of myself in some high-toned theatrical she hopes to bring to Fortune."

"Oh?" Amy's eyes crinkled. She'd probably guessed from the start that Evelina's reluctant cad had been her son. "Vanilla? How nice." She winked at Evelina, took the white freezer bag and sailed into the kitchen.

Ryan shifted from one foot to the other and measured Evelina through half-closed eyes. He looked like the impossibly virile male model in a cigarette ad. "How'd you track me down?" he asked.

Track him down? He was even more egotistical than she'd supposed. She picked up her purse and set it on the couch behind her, stalling for time. She didn't want to snarl at him. He was Amy's son, after all.

"Believe it or not, my being here is a coincidence."

One eyebrow peaked and the other lowered. He hooked a thumb in the pocket of his jeans. The sexual candor of his gaze disturbed her. Yet she didn't even know why she defined it as sexual. His eyes didn't roam the length of her and back again. They didn't linger on her breasts. They mostly remained on her face. Yet every hill and valley of her body reacted with a hot tingling sensation that seemed to come from a bed of burning coals deep inside her.

"You don't believe me?" she asked, injecting firmness into her voice.

"I will if you want me to."

"I asked Calvin if he knew of someone who'd be willing to let us take up space for rehearsals. He suggested your mother." Evelina's mouth felt parched. If she'd had a pitcher of water handy she could have drained it dry. "That is, I didn't know Amy was your mother until you walked in."

"Good old Calvin and his practical jokes. That's one I owe him. I suppose he told you I'd be a pushover for whatever Ma wants. That I'd agree to join the cast if she asked me."

"Well, no. Like I said, I didn't know she was your mother."

Ryan snatched an apple from a blue-and-white ceramic bowl sitting on the dining-room table, tossed it from one hand to the other and polished it on his shirt-front. "Ma was tickled pink about your idea, I gather?"

"Yes, Ma was," Amy said, coming in from the kitchen with a bowl of salad. "You aren't going to eat that apple, are you, Ryan? You'll spoil your appetite. We eat in five minutes."

"Nothing spoils my appetite."

"I can attest to that," Evelina muttered under her breath.

Dinner was spaghetti with a bottled sauce. But with Amy's additions of spices and onions and other good things, it had a homemade taste that called for second helpings. Dessert, the ice cream Ryan had brought home, would come later in the evening when their stomachs had more room.

While Amy and Evelina put the kitchen in order, Ryan went to work unsticking a kitchen window whose frame had been painted so often it wouldn't open and close properly. Then Amy offered to make phone calls to friends who might be receptive to Evelina's ideas. She'd invite them over the next day for tryouts.

"We'll make an occasion of it," she said, her enthusiasm bubbling over. "Everyone can bring a covered dish."

"Can it be managed on such short notice?"

"Leave it to me." Amy beamed. "You can hand out the scripts after we eat, listen to the readings and award the parts to those who're best qualified."

"It sounds super. If you don't think it'll be too much trouble for you..."

Ryan paused in his paint-scraping and jerked his head toward his mother. "She's Wonder Woman, didn't you know?" His tight-lipped delivery hinted that his comment was more sarcastic than jovial.

"If it was too much trouble, I wouldn't have offered." Amy opened a drawer in the telephone stand and brought out an address book. "Now that you're finished, Ryan, I can get started."

"Who says I'm finished?"

"I won't be able to make myself heard with that racket. Why don't you show Evelina around the ranch? Then the two of you can pick blackberries to go with the ice cream. I've a notion Calvin will show up later to see how things have worked out."

"You can bank on it." Ryan exhaled in exasperation. "Okay. Let me wash up, and we'll be on our way."

"Meanwhile I'll get Evelina settled."

The guest room was large, airy and bright, papered in shades of yellow and orange, with the canopied bed covered by a handmade quilt done in the painstaking flower-garden pattern. A frame with another quilt in progress stood in one corner. A crammed sewing basket with a partly embroidered dresser scarf lay on the padded window seat.

"Excuse the clutter." Amy scooped a well-worn book off the bed.

A snapshot fluttered to the floor and Evelina picked it up. The woman in the picture was a much younger Amy, with lots of black hair fixed in the exuberant bouffant style of the fifties. A man wearing a squashed hat perched jauntily on his head and a smile very much like Ryan's stood with his arm around her. Amy looked happy and very much in love. Her head rested on his shoulder.

"Ryan's father," Amy said, as if it weren't obvious.

"He's handsome."

"He was a charmer." Amy took the snapshot from Evelina and gazed at it with moist eyes. "He looked like such a rogue. No one would have taken him for a poet."

"That's true." Evelina conjured up a picture of Ryan in a toga, spouting Shakespeare.

"Oh, I don't mean he made a living that way. Few people can. He was a salesman before he took up ranching, and a good one. But in private, just for himself—and for me. He wrote beautiful verses." Amy plucked a slim green book from a shelf next to the door and laid it on the night table. "He had some of them privately printed and dedicated to me."

Was. Had. Past tense. How long had she been widowed? The pain of her husband's loss seemed fresh. But then, theirs had evidently been too special a love to be easily forgotten.

"That must have made you proud," Evelina said gently.

"Oh, yes." The woman touched loving fingertips to the fragile gold lettering on the book's cover. "I'll leave it here. You might like to glance through it. Sometimes reading helps to..." Her voice fell, as she abandoned what she was about to say.

Evelina swallowed. "Yes, it does," she said, without really knowing what she was agreeing to. "Thank you."

"We all have our private pleasures, don't we?" The brightness returned to Amy's voice. "Our special abilities and, in some cases, vices. My ability is sewing. I made that quilt, you know."

"It's exquisite. Such a lot of work!"

"I don't consider it work. It's fun. So are making graduation dresses and bridal gowns. Even doing alterations. All of it makes me feel creative."

"I can appreciate that. With the kind of work I do, I'm in constant need of costumes."

"What do you do?"

"I teach modern dance at a high school in Houston. We put on a May Fete every year and a Christmas pageant. The girls love to be onstage. We also have programs at the local community center, where I'm a volunteer."

"And now Fortune is lucky enough to have you." Amy beamed. "Is Faye a teacher as well?"

"No, but the Good Fortune celebration was her idea."

"Ah. Talent runs in the family. She and Kurt live pretty far from town, so I've only met her a few times. But as I recall, she doesn't look at all like you."

"We're complete opposites." Evelina shook away the image of her and Faye standing side by side for comparison. "She's never done anything like this before and had no idea how much work it entailed. Then unexpectedly, her name was drawn in a contest she'd entered when Kurt bought some heavy equipment. She won a Mediterranean cruise."

"She must have been thrilled."

"Yes. But the timing is all wrong. The cruise overlaps with time that should be spent in rehearsal and preparation for the celebration."

"So she sent an SOS and you came to the rescue."

"That's about it."

"I understand she's from Austin," Amy mused. "But you're from Houston?"

"I grew up in Austin, too. I had to relocate when I took the teaching job." Evelina didn't add that her move had been made to put distance between her and her sister. It had grown too uncomfortable sitting across the table from Kurt and Faye at family dinners, with all the sympathetic looks and with "Poor Evelina" hanging, unspoken, in the air.

"You'll be glad you came here," Amy pronounced. "People are warm and friendly."

Evelina nodded her agreement, even though she wasn't all that sure people were. "I only wish you were closer to Houston. I'm always in dire need of a good seamstress. I try to keep dancing costumes in stock sizes for practice sessions, as well as for recitals, but..."

"Oh, please." Amy's eyes danced with excitement at the prospect. "I can sew for you. With the new expressway, I won't be all that far away. In fact, if you give me measurements, we can do it by mail."

"Are you sure?" Evelina would have thought that the workings of the ranch would take up too much of her time.

"I can hardly wait. Here. Let me show you my current project."

It was a quilt done entirely in white—backing, appliqué and decorative stitching. The amount of work that must have gone into the intricate all-over pattern of leaves, flowers and birds was staggering. Evelina was speechless.

"This is a bride's quilt," Amy said, arranging an end of the fabric into a smoother fold. "For Ryan's wife-to-be. What do you think?"

"It...it's the most beautiful quilt I've ever seen," Evelina heard herself saying as if from somewhere far-off. "She'll love it."

"Oh, I hope so. I'm almost finished. And none too soon."

Evelina tried to tighten her hands into fists, but her fingers felt like globs of gelatin. Ryan's wife-to-be. She might have known.

CHAPTER FOUR

"OVER HERE WE HAVE chickens." Grasping Evelina's elbow, Ryan led her to the coop for a closer inspection.

"I wondered what those feathery little creatures were," she said, feeling more confident now. In the minutes she'd taken to freshen up, she'd retwisted her hair in a way that left it looking much smoother, with a fetching tendril, the color of maple syrup, over each ear. She'd removed all traces of streaked mascara and reapplied her lip gloss. Now she smelled of scented soap, instead of road dust.

"Leghorns. They supply fresh breakfast eggs for us and our neighbors."

"Lucky neighbors."

"The bearded fellow is a goat." Still holding her elbow, he led her closer to the slat-board running pen. "He's a member of the family."

"I can see the resemblance."

A whinny from the stables came right on cue.

"Horses." He stood back to allow her to enter first.

"I wondered what they were."

Was Ryan's fiancée the reason he refused to take part in the melodrama? Was the woman a sophisticate who would consider it beneath his dignity? Where was she now? Did she live in Fortune?

What possible difference did it make?

Two beautifully groomed animals, one chestnut and the other white with a black-spotted rump, came to the front of their stalls for attention. Ryan stroked each of them in turn. "Salome and Dan," he said.

"They're magnificent."

"They are that. Would you care to ride while you're here?"

The woman he planned to marry was undoubtedly an expert horsewoman. Evelina pictured her fashion-model tall, with high cheekbones and gleaming long black hair. Her figure, in her neat riding habit, would be slim and her hips nonexistent.

"I've never been on a horse in my life," she admitted. "I'm from the city, remember?"

Ryan laughed, allowing her a glimpse of white squarish teeth and the single deepening dimple. "They don't have horses in Houston?"

"Of course," she said, feeling foolish. "But there weren't any places to ride near where I lived. I never got around to learning."

"Too busy dancing?"

Was she imagining the twinge of disdain in his voice? "Why do I get the impression you don't approve of dancing?"

"How could I disapprove? It's just that when their chores are done, kids should be outside playing baseball or..." A brushing gesture with one hand indicated that the list of alternative pastimes was endless.

Reaching overhead, he took two metal pails off a shelf and handed one to her. "For the berries. We'll have a contest and see who picks the most."

"You're on," Evelina agreed.

They moved past an assortment of pens and corrals, then a yard where two ranch hands were having trouble leading a feisty cinnamon colt into a trailer. At a fork in the walkway, Ryan guided her to the left, past rows of hollyhocks and a squared-off kitchen garden, with plantings of radishes, squash and tomatoes, to a meadow where seas of golden grasses were allowed to grow long and tangle as they wished. A narrow footpath ran through it to a wooded section beyond.

"I didn't know you were so gung ho for outdoor exercise," Evelina said, still musing over his dismissal of dancing. "What kind do *you* do?"

His eyes twinkled with amusement. "You can look around and actually ask that question?"

"These days when cowboys aren't using helicopters, they ride from one section to the other in a pickup. Besides, when you ride horseback, the horse gets all the exercise."

His laugh was explosive. "Spoken like a city girl!"

The path widened and they were able to walk side by side. Their easy swinging movements brought thighs, arms and hips into brief but disturbing contact. Evelina realized her awareness of that contact was all out of proportion....

She remembered feeling like this only once before. In the ninth grade, a boy she'd adored from a distance for a very long time actually asked if he could walk her home from school. As he took her books, their fingers touched, and the touching had been like an electric shock. She'd almost gasped.

What was his name? Vincent? Victor? She couldn't recall. And so it would be someday with Ryan Garrison. "He was terribly attractive," she imagined herself telling a friend years from now. "But I can't, for the life of me, remember his name."

As they approached a meandering stone wall, Ryan swung over it effortlessly, then reached back to help her. She could have managed it alone easily. But she didn't say so. She wanted to feel her hand in his, as well as bask in the smile he gave her in accompaniment.

"Up you go."

She waited for her senses to hit the ground, along with her feet, before she spoke. "Thank you." Even though Ryan was spoken for, she was still glad she'd come to Fortune.

Brown-and-gold butterflies flitting here and there, grasshoppers chirping and the smell of wild grapes nudged an armload of pleasant memories out of their hiding places. She thought back to when she was small and her grandparents were alive. She and her sister, Faye, had spent two weeks one summer at their ranch. That was before she and Faye had become antagonists.

They'd been close once, hadn't they? Or had there always been a sense of competition? Competition in which Faye had been a clear winner.

"So close in age. Only a year apart," people would say. "But they hardly even look like sisters."

It didn't matter. She'd always known Faye was prettier—and smarter.

Vance. That was the name of the boy who'd offered to carry her books home from school. She remembered something else, too. As they walked together that long ago day, he'd bombarded her with questions. Would Faye be home when they got there? Did Faye date much? Was there anyone special in Faye's life?

Faye, Faye, Faye. Vance had only used her to get closer to her sister.

Evelina had stopped walking, her face so feverish she knew it must have been scarlet. She'd snatched her books away from him and ran, barely getting out of his sight before she threw up in a vacant lot.

There'd been other times, too. Times when—

No! It was much too lovely an evening to dwell on ancient tragedy. She was happy with her life now—and content. Maybe the man walking beside her wasn't *her* Mr. Right—he was someone else's—but she liked his company, nevertheless.

She liked his walk, too. It wasn't a swagger as she'd first thought. It was carefree and at the same time purposeful. She liked his confident jaw, his strong nose and generous mouth. There was even a comfortable camaraderie in his teasing.

"Here we have the woods," he said.

"How can we see it with all these trees?" She grimaced at her weak joke and laughed when he grimaced, too.

They entered what was almost a different world. It wasn't a deep dark woods, but had the feel of a fairyland. She didn't imagine there were many woods like these in this part of Texas. The sun found its way through the overhead canopy of leaves easily to send dust-speckled shafts of light to the spongy floor. Something skittered—a rabbit, perhaps—across their path.

"You don't look like a dancer," Ryan said suddenly.

Her pulses quickened. "Because I'm short and chubby?"

"Chubby?" He spoke slowly, as if relishing the sound of the word. "Whereabouts?"

He caught her wrist, pushed her slightly ahead and fastened his gaze on her behind. "Maybe a little. In all the right places."

She pulled away with more vehemence than she'd intended, hating her overreaction. She wasn't overweight, but she had been in her teens. It was a self-image not easily dispelled.

"I didn't mean it as an insult."

"I didn't take it as one."

Ryan snorted, clearly guessing he'd hit a nerve. "The hell you didn't."

"Where are these blackberries of yours?" She lifted her chin in defiance as she leapt into another subject.

"Patience. Did you expect to find supermarket counters with stacks of little wooden boxes?"

His expression said that he was thinking something else—just as she was. Was he wondering if he should wrap his arms around her and kiss her until she had no breath left for argument? It was probably his experience that women clung to him, weak and submissive, ready to say yes to whatever he wanted....

"You don't look like a cowboy either," she said suddenly.

"I don't?"

"You look more like—" she touched a finger to her lips "—a private eye. No. An airplane pilot."

"This is your captain speaking," he said in a deep resonant voice as if trying on the profession for size.

"Not that kind of pilot. The kind who has a plane of his own. One held together with tape. He picks up passengers in the middle of a swamp in the dead of night and flies them out of the country."

"You see?" He grinned crookedly. "I don't mind being insulted."

"A soldier of fortune."

"A villain?"

"Exactly."

He was more than just attractive, she admitted, as her irritation calmed. He was charming without trying to be. She'd dated a number of attractive men, and none had affected her as Ryan did. He seemed to say, *This is what I am. Take it or leave it.*

Had she truly been in love with Kurt? How could she have been, when his presence had never filled her, enveloped her and probed its way to the core of her femininity as the presence of this comparative stranger was doing? It seemed she hadn't affected Kurt that way, either.

"I feel comfortable with you," Kurt used to say. "I can be myself. You never make me feel I have to prove myself. Actually, you're like a best friend."

He hadn't even expected her to be hurt when he told her about Faye. He'd thought his joy would be hers.

"Dead ahead," Ryan announced as they approached a clearing, jarring her back to the present.

"Aha!" She saw them at the same time. Bushes. At least a dozen of them, so heavily laden with fat purplish berries their branches dipped to the ground.

As he pushed aside a tree branch, the leaves rustled. There was a bird cry and a flash of scarlet. Evelina threw up an arm to shade her eyes.

"A redbird. He's beautiful."

"We have a saying in these parts," Ryan drawled. "See a redbird before sunset, and you'll be kissed twice before nightfall."

"Twice," she echoed disbelievingly.

"Twice."

"That's hardly likely."

His grin was maddeningly inviting. "You're with a villain, remember? I might take advantage of you."

She bit her lower lip, wishing she could find a witty riposte. But what? She jabbed him in the ribs with her elbow. "Are we having this berry-picking contest or aren't we?"

He pretended to double over with the force of the blow. "We are."

"Then let's go."

Obviously she was going to win. He kept making teasing remarks that made her laugh. Not only that, he ate as many of the berries as he dropped into his pail. Coming close, he peered at her pickings.

"I hope you know that the deciding factor is quality, not quantity. I pick only the sweetest, juiciest ones. Here." He popped one into her mouth.

"Delicious," she said, when she was able to speak.

"Like I said. Quality."

"Nice try. But I distinctly remember your saying whoever picks the most."

"Leave it to me to draw an opponent with a good memory."

Laughing, she thrust a hand through the lowest branches to a hidden place where she'd spotted enough berries to make several handfuls and force him to concede. A thorn bit into her finger and she cried out in pain.

"Let me see that." Ryan dragged her to her feet and contemplated the finger where a drop of blood oozed through the skin. "That's what you get for being greedy."

"Greedy?" she sputtered.

Still holding the injured digit, he snaked his free arm around her waist and pulled her toward him, onto her toes and off balance, giving him full advantage. Before she realized what he planned, he kissed her on the mouth.

It was a brief hard kiss, full of fire and madness. She almost dropped her pail as pleasure coursed through her, making her feel she would drown in it.

"Is that better?" he asked solicitously.

"Is it..." She fought the impulse to relax against him. He belonged to someone else. He was teasing. And if he wasn't, he was contemptible.

If contempt was all she felt for him, she'd be in a better position. "Aren't you supposed to kiss the finger?"

"You kiss what *you* want, and I'll kiss what *I* want," he returned.

"Not a logical answer."

"It doesn't work directly. It's based on acupressure."

"Like massaging your earlobe to cure a toothache."

"Right. It's very scientific." Still holding her captive, he dipped his head again and brushed his mouth against her ear.

She set her teeth together to still the primitive thrill that zigzagged through her, knowing she should pull away from him, laugh and make some lighthearted remark to let him know she recognized the joke. "I don't have a toothache," she said.

"You see? It works."

His shirt gapped as he held her, allowing her a glimpse of the dark curling hair on his chest. A glimpse that filled her with an all but irresistible compulsion to thrust her fingers through the shadowy tangle.

"That isn't why you kissed me," she accused.

"No, it isn't."

"You wanted to make your local saying come true. About the redbird."

"Right."

"I think we have enough," she said falteringly, the strength she'd meant to convey evaporating somewhere between her throat and her lips.

"Speak for yourself."

"I meant—" she jerked the pail upward "—enough berries."

"I know what you meant."

Was he going to kiss her again? Her lips prickled with anticipation. A dog barked somewhere in the distance, helping to distract her. With the distraction came an attack of common sense and a replay of Amy's words.

Ryan's wife-to-be.

Whoever the woman was, she trusted him. Evelina saw herself in juxtaposition with his faceless fiancée. She saw Kurt and Faye exchanging looks of longing. Saw them kissing in the shadows, while she sat home, oblivious to what was going on.

"Will I meet your fiancée?" she asked sharply, bending farther back than was comfortable in an attempt to avoid further contact with him. "Maybe she'd like a part in the play."

"Who?" He straightened and allowed her to do the same. A sheen of perspiration glistened on his forehead. One shaggy brow lifted and the other lowered.

"Your mother told me about your wife-to-be."

"She did?" He was hedging. Trying to think of a face-saving comment, no doubt. "Why don't *you* tell me about her?"

Had she sounded accusing? She hoped not. She wouldn't want him to think it mattered to her that he wasn't available. "Amy showed me the bride's quilt she's making. Such delicate work."

"The quilt." He nodded. "It so happens that it's for *if*, not *when*. Ever heard of a hope chest?"

"Yes, but..." Evelina blinked, confused now. "But what?"

"It's supposed to be the woman who keeps one."

Though the sun was going down, the air was as hot and sultry as midday. He clapped a hand to the back of his neck and rubbed, as he might at an insect bite. "Ma didn't have any daughters. And in this case, the hope is hers. Not mine."

"I see." Her smile didn't even *feel* convincing.

He squinted one eye. "If you thought I was attached, why did you kiss me that way?"

"I think you're mixed up about who kissed who."

"Maybe we're both mixed up."

She stared back at him for a moment before deciding to let the matter stand. The hunger in the meeting of their mouths had been undeniably shared. To argue otherwise would only have left her open to ridicule.

Pulling herself up with new dignity, she started away too quickly. Her foot slipped off the beaten path and sank into the softer woodland floor, twisting, and setting her off balance.

Though he'd probably considered allowing her to fall on her self-righteous little fanny, he caught her shoulders and set her right. "You should have worn something meant for walking. Those shoes are all straps."

"Cowboy boots?"

"Why not? They're practical."

She shot him a sideways glance. "I didn't expect to go hiking when I dressed this morning."

"It's good to be prepared." He kept an arm around her even after they began walking again, as if wanting to feel the muscles, tendons, all the bits and pieces of woman that made up Evelina Pettit, moving under his fingers.

She didn't attempt to wriggle out of his grasp. Would he have allowed it if she had?

Her hair had fallen into disarray again during the berry picking. He was eyeing the strands that had begun to slip from the pins at the nape of her neck as though he planned to smooth them. If he did, she'd probably react by leaping out of her skin.

Instead of waiting for it to happen, she dug into her repertoire of questions for a few that might put their conversation back on buddy-buddy lines. Probably hoping for the same thing, Ryan told her about Thomas Tully, his great-great-grandfather on his mother's side who'd come from Massachusetts when he was sixteen to work as a chuck-line rider until he'd saved enough to buy the land for the original Tully T and two breed heifers. Then he'd sent for a mail-order bride.

The land and the cows first, Evelina mused. Then the bride. "So the Tully T Ranch has been in your mother's family for generations?"

"Since 1892, to be exact. In those days good pastureland went for only a few dollars an acre."

According to Ryan, Amy's grandfather, Thomas Tully, Jr., took over the ranch and expanded it, when Thomas, Sr., died at ninety-nine. He'd been the one who taught Ryan that a smart cowboy was always gentle with the animals. It paid off in the long run.

Ryan plucked at a twig that had snagged in Evelina's hair and fingered it absently as they continued on their way. "I loved that old man. Before he would teach me to ride, he taught me to fall. I'd be doing a fierce lot of it before I was saddle broke, he'd say, and I'd better get the hang of it right off.''

Despite his grandfather's attempts to instill a love of ranching in him, Ryan developed a passion for mechanics, instead. By the time he was fourteen, he could take a car apart and put it back together better than it was before he started. He'd expected to get into a line of work that would allow him to make a profit out of this hobby.

"I was sick to death of the ranch. There were too many ups and downs in the cattle market. Too much depended on things beyond my control."

And Ryan was a man who needed to be in control. "Such as the weather?" Evelina asked.

"Exactly."

Then, while he was attending college at his mother's insistence, one of the supposed dry oil wells her father had left to her turned into a gusher. At first, Ryan saw it as his chance to escape. To start up in the city and invest in a service station or two.

"But in the end, I couldn't."

"You missed the dust devils and armadillos?"

"Maybe. I realized that I wasn't just staying on at the ranch to please Ma." He shrugged one shoulder. "Even given the highs and lows of living off the land, Fortune—the ranch—is home."

Trying to recuperate from the mixed emotions that had bedeviled her since she'd met Ryan, Evelina was listening with only half an ear when something yanked at her wrist. "Wait!" she cried, stopping short.

"Now what?"

"My charm is caught."

"Your what?"

As usual she was wearing her lucky bracelet. It was fashioned of gold links and held a single charm—a glass slipper, which had tangled in the branches of an ambitious young sycamore.

"Why would you wear something like that on a hike through the woods?" He moved to disentangle her.

"I can do it," she protested.

"Not one-handed." He brushed her efforts away as he had when he'd operated on her eye, and held the wrist so that she was behind him. He worked carefully, ignoring her wriggling and her gasps as he bent the wood, tore away a leaf or two and freed her. "There you go."

"Thank you," she said, inspecting the bracelet to make sure it was intact. Another two hundred yards and they'd be in the meadow again, in sight of the house. She took a step.

"Hold on a minute," he said. The expression on his face was the same one he'd worn just before he'd kissed her.

She swallowed hard, waiting.

He closed the gap between them, but she stepped back, opening it again.

He took another step, and so did she. "Is something wrong with my hair?"

"Nope."

"My...face?" She touched a hand to it.

"Nope."

"Ryan." Another step wedged her against a tree.

She wasn't going anywhere and she knew it. "It's a real pretty trinket," he said. "It suits you."

She fluttered unsure fingers to the glass slipper and set it swinging. "My sister gave it to me when I graduated from high school. Cinderella was my favorite story character, you see. She meant it partly as teasing. I used to daydream a lot."

"That's not surprising."

There was barely an inch between them now. He pressed forward, anyway, angling his head to ensure their lips' perfect melding.

His mouth was incredibly warm, moist and giving, assailing her senses till she was all but overcome with the desire to knead the hard muscles of his back with her fingers, to comb through the darkness of his hair and to hold him fast until she'd had her fill.

When their mouths drew apart, they still stood together as if separating was an impossibility.

"The redbird," she whispered.

"Twice before sunset," he added. Then they started to walk again.

Ahead, a gray squirrel skittered halfway down a peeling elm, clung to its trunk upside down and scolded noisily.

"Do you think he's upset because we're taking some of his berries?" she asked.

"Likely he wants a handful of hickory nuts as a toll for our trespassing."

Another squirrel appeared, chattered at the first and chased it into the brush.

"I like your woods." Evelina swiped at the bits of dried grass that clung to her pants. "How exciting it must have been for you as a child."

"I played cowboys and Indians among these trees many a time."

"You? Played make-believe?" She pretended to be shocked at his revelation.

"Yep." He shrugged. "But I gave it up. How about you?"

She didn't answer. A station wagon was parked in the driveway of the Garrison house. "You have company."

"Calvin. Come to see Ma. Poor fellow."

"Why do you say that?"

"Because he's wasting his time."

"You mean Calvin from the café and Amy?" She smiled at the idea.

"You find that comical? Because he doesn't look like the hero in a TV soap opera?"

"Because, well, in a way, yes. I don't mean his physical appearance, exactly. It's just that he doesn't strike me as the romantic type."

"The romantic type." Ryan kicked at a half-buried rock that lay in his path as if it had insulted him. "Calvin might not offer to climb the highest mountain or swim the deepest river, but he was there when Ma needed him. He helped her through the lean times. Lending money for feed bills and mortgage payments. Fixing fences. Putting on a new roof."

"Sounds as if he's been a good friend."

"Good friend is right."

"But Amy is a vibrant, attractive woman. She might want something more."

"Someone who writes poetry, for instance?"

His father had been a poet, according to Amy. Why did he sound so bitter? "Maybe."

Amy was standing on the front porch talking to her visitor. She looked toward the meadow and waved. Calvin waved, too. His hair rose in sandy tufts where he'd run a hand through it for want of a comb. His pants were ill-fitting and baggy, his shirt, faded and rumpled.

Ryan shook his head. "He's a damn good man and he cares for her."

"Cares. That's not the same thing as being in love."

"Genuine caring is a helluva lot more important," Ryan growled, walking faster.

She released the sigh that had been building up inside her. It wasn't enough that she was allowing herself to fall for a man she hardly knew. She was falling for a man who was as romantic as an old shoe.

No. Not a shoe, she thought grimly. A cowboy boot.

CHAPTER FIVE

A TAP AT THE DOOR jarred Evelina awake. She brought an arm over her eyes to shield them from the rays of morning sun that had found their way through the slats of the blinds she'd neglected to close the night before.

"Evelina?" Amy called.

She yawned. "I'm awake."

"Busy day ahead. Rise and shine."

Deciding that the already-soaring temperature called for an action-geared hairstyle, Evelina pulled her hair into a lush and bouncy ponytail.

She'd made pin curls over each ear before she'd gone to bed the night before, hoping to fashion soft, waving tendrils. The effect was more perky than glamorous.

"Your hair is by far your best feature," Faye was fond of telling her. "It's so healthy-looking."

Her best feature? Maybe she should have combed it over her face.

Healthy-looking? A prize cow was healthy-looking.

Better to have a lithe and seductive figure, or an interesting artist's model's bone structure that caught light and shadow dramatically.

The sleeveless cotton shirt in a bright coral print she decided to wear for her meeting with prospective cast members wasn't glamorous, either, but it was cool and went well with the almond-colored linen skirt she'd pressed the night before.

Thinking of what Ryan had said about Calvin taking a fancy to Amy, she'd spent the evening watching surreptitiously for any longing looks the would-be suitor might have fastened on the supposed object of his affections. She'd listened, too, for any extravagant compliments he might have paid in his efforts at courtship. Once, Calvin told Amy that the perfume she was wearing made his nose itch. Then he told her about a new recipe he had for Brunswick stew that would run rings around hers. When he was leaving, he stood in the doorway complaining about the service he'd been getting from the bread man at the café.

This was Ryan's idea of a budding relationship between a man and a woman? Then there was Ryan himself.

At one point in the evening, Ryan, Amy and Calvin had played an animated game of pick-up-sticks in the kitchen. Giving no quarter to anyone, Ryan had won all the matches. Did he excel in everything? She knew he had a steady hand. His expertise in flicking the stray eyelash from her eye and then untangling her glass slipper from the branch in the woods proved that.

The woods. A flux of mind-blowing images swept through her mind when she thought about it. These same images had fed her dreams the night before and would feed many more in the weeks ahead if she didn't put up a courageous battle. And she would. There was room for only one king-size disappointment in anyone's life, and she'd already had hers with Kurt.

The sound of hammering drew her to the window now, and she pulled aside the curtain to see Ryan on the far side of the chicken coop, mending a broken rail in the fence that separated two of the corrals.

He'd taken off his shirt, and she could see that his back was impossibly broad and sun-bronzed, as she'd known it would be. The play of his muscles as he worked, bending and stretching, climbing and reaching, was so intriguing, she would have stayed and watched if Amy hadn't been waiting.

Considering how close she had come to losing her glass slipper the day before, she decided to leave it on the dresser. She dug into her suitcase for a chunky bracelet of multicolored beads, instead. Since she'd been a toddler, she felt naked without something pretty around her wrist. Something to touch when she was nervous or deep in thought.

After wriggling her feet into a pair of canvas sneakers, she went to join her hostess for breakfast.

Amy was on the telephone, talking animatedly about the afternoon tryouts and her part in the preparations.

"I have no idea when it will all be over," she was saying. "But Evvie will be exhausted. Maybe I can convince her to stay over another night. I'd love having her. Oh. Wait. Here she is now."

"Who is it?" Evelina mouthed silently as Amy presented her with the the phone.

"Your sister."

"Faye?" Evelina marveled as she held the receiver to her ear. "How did you know I was here?"

"You have got to be kidding. The way news travels in Fortune, I'm sure everybody knows your astrological sign and what you eat for breakfast. I hear you're already set up at the Tully T."

"Yes, I am. Amy Garrison is an angel. Now I'm waiting for the producer and director. How soon can you get here?"

There was a thump and a groan. Faye dropped the telephone. "Today? Now, you mean?"

"Well, not next week."

Evelina bit back her irritation. This pilgrimage to Fortune had not been her idea. She'd been lassoed and roped into it. Faye and Kurt had been married only a little over a year when he told Faye about his yearning to return to Fortune and the simple ranch life of his youth. Bored with her bookkeeping job, Faye had envisioned a quaint, Hollywood-movie-set Western town. There'd be hayrides, box socials and weekly dances at the town hall, where lanky cowpokes would fight for a place on her dance card. Kurt would be the envy of everyone. Faye would be caught in a whirlwind of social activity, and other wives would come to her for advice on fashion and makeup.

Reality was quite different.

There'd been no welcome wagons, clubs or committees. The single one-screen movie theater wasn't even open most of the time. To make matters worse, Faye was convinced the longtime residents resented her.

The idea for a Return to Good Fortune gala had come to her in the middle of the night, and she'd called Evelina long-distance. She would base her musical presentation on *Here's Texas,* a recital Evelina had put together to showcase her students.

Naturally Faye would rewrite to give the characters more scope. The songs and situations would be given more sophistication. She'd been involved in amateur theatricals in college, and this would be a snap. People, wanting to be part of it, would be drawn to her.

Still half-asleep, Evelina had praised the brilliant idea, wished her sister luck and gone back to sleep.

A week later the second phone call had come.

"I can't do it, stuck way out here. The stupid truck only has a stick shift. Can you imagine anything so primitive? Kurt calls my idea 'hogwash,' and tells me to stop pestering his friends. Can you imagine Kurt even using the term 'hogwash'? Evelina, I need you."

"You always say that the word 'can't' isn't in your vocabulary," Evelina had said.

"It is now. Besides, you're used to organizing these things. I'm not."

"There was a first time for me, too," Evelina had reminded her. "I was shaking in my shoes. Go for it."

The third phone call had been edged with hysteria. According to Faye, nothing was going right, even though she'd been working like a demon. She'd spent hours in the library with old newspaper microfilm, digging out historical facts about her adopted town. She'd revised Evelina's script, typed it and made photocopies. She'd worked out expenses on paper. She'd secured permission for the songs that were incorporated into the story. She'd contacted a fiddler, who said he could get a Western band together with two weeks' notice, along with a square-dance caller. She'd even spoken with Patrick Hayes, the lead dancer from the Houston-based troupe that periodically tried out new routines at the community center.

When Evelina's determination to stay out of it didn't waver, Faye had dropped the bomb. She'd wanted to wait to spring the news, but she couldn't. It seemed that she'd accompanied Kurt to Waco one day when he was looking at new machinery for the ranch. Bored, she'd entered her name in a draw, not expecting to win. But she had. A fourteen-day luxury cruise that would take them from Sicily to Corfu to Venice and points between.

"It'll be like the *Love Boat*," Faye had gone on. "The honeymoon Kurt and I never had."

"You had a honeymoon."

"In San Antonio? Where the high point is a tour of the Alamo?"

"I'm happy for you, honey," Evelina had said. "But don't they have different dates to choose from for these tours? To give winners a chance to make arrangements to get away?"

"They do. But this is the only time Kurt can manage with his schedule." She sighed. "I've been holding off telling you. For a couple of reasons."

"Such as?"

"Mom thought you might . . . well, be jealous. You know how you always say good things drop in my lap?"

"I can't remember saying that." Evelina set her teeth together. She might have thought it at times, but she hadn't said it.

"And then there's Kurt. He actually wanted me to withdraw my name as prize winner. He said he couldn't get away that long. The ranch would fall apart without him."

"Would it?"

Faye groaned. "He took over an already-working spread. The foreman has been here for more years than Kurt's been alive. And the hands are experienced. Kurt said he'd make it up to me when we're more settled. Settled, of all things. I thought, when? When we're ninety-five? I couldn't imagine his ever finding time to take me to to Capri or Pompeii."

Not wanting to take sides in their argument, Evelina hadn't commented.

Mentally she'd clicked off the dates Faye mentioned. "That'll still give you time to throw things together when you return. Especially if you have your cast members chosen and they have scripts to study while you're gone."

"I don't want to throw things together. There are people here who would love to see me fall on my face."

"I'm sure you're mistaken."

"Besides, it'll involve far more rehearsal than I'd anticipated." Faye must have cupped her hands around the receiver. Her next words came in a kind of echo. "Most of them can't put two words together without stuttering. It would be a disaster."

"Well, don't expect too much. They aren't professionals, after all. But I'm sorry I can't help. I just can't get away."

"That's final?"

"Final." Evelina had gripped the telephone, fighting her inborn habit of giving in to her sister's tears. "Say hello to Kurt for me, will you? And have a fantastic time on your cruise."

Even as she'd settled the receiver on the hook, she knew she hadn't won the war, even if she'd won this battle.

The next call had come from her mother. Mrs. Pettit started in the usual way, talking in her small and breathy voice about the problems they'd had with the suicidal drivers on a Massachusetts highway. Then she was quiet, gearing up for what Evelina knew what was coming.

"Are you sure you aren't staying away from Fortune for other reasons besides your job?"

"What reasons are those?"

"Couldn't it be that you're still hurt and angry about...about Faye's stealing Kurt away from you?"

"I'm not hurt and I'm not angry. Not anymore. Truly."

"I'm glad to hear that." Mrs. Pettit hadn't sounded convinced. "Then what's the problem? School will be out."

"Yes, but I still have the center."

"You don't even get paid for that." Mrs. Pettit employed her resigned voice, very much like Faye. "If you can't or won't do this thing, your father and I will have to cancel the rest of our trip and come home. I don't know anything about putting on a show, but your sister needs somebody on her side."

She has Kurt, Evelina was tempted to say. But that would only have reinforced everybody's belief that she was acting out of spite.

How could she let her parents cancel their trip? For the last five years before his retirement, her father had talked about how he was going to make up for all the vacations they hadn't been able to take. He was going to buy a camper and see the country, state by state. For the last year, he'd pored over maps and travel brochures. His dream was finally coming true. How could she spoil it?

So now, here Evelina was in Fortune, with odds more than even that she'd be handling the big celebration alone.

"You can't imagine how busy I've been," Faye went on. "I finally convinced Kurt that this cruise is something I need and deserve. But we leave Tuesday. The heat here is so unbearable I'm sick to my stomach most of the time. And if I'm all worn-out, how can I have any fun?"

"In other words, you aren't coming to the tryouts."

"You don't need me. I sent you the scripts and the audiotapes. It's all in a day's work for you, isn't it?"

"Oh, Faye—"

"Great!" Apparently Faye sensed victory and allowed a bit of animation to color her voice. "I knew I could count on you. By the way, Amy wants you to stay over again tonight and drive here in the morning. It's for the best. Kurt painted your room, and the smell will be gone by then. You can fill me in, and I'll model my new Mediterranean wardrobe for you."

Evelina could hardly wait.

The day was humid, but it was pleasant and breezy under the trees where Calvin and Ryan had set up tables and folding chairs. The first guest arrived at about twelve-thirty. Right on time. Less than fifteen minutes later, thanks to Amy's friendly persuasion, the road was lined with cars belonging to enthusiastic participants.

The food was wonderful. There was sweet homegrown corn with butter. There were sliced tomatoes like none she'd ever tasted, salads of every imaginable sort and two huge platters of cold cuts. Amy had wheedled watermelons out of a farmer down the road, and there was an enormous bowl of grape punch with plenty more left in the kitchen for refilling.

All that was missing was Ryan. He and his truck had hightailed it to the neighboring town of Jasper. He hadn't even been at the breakfast table. According to Amy, he'd promised to drive an old friend of hers, Sissy Fox, to the vet's. The woman had an old retriever who was ailing.

"Poor Sissy has no husband, no children—no one," Amy said. "I'm only glad we can help her out now and then."

Evelina nodded and said she understood. But she'd have bet almost anything that Ryan would have signed up for a sail on the *Titanic* to avoid being home today of all days.

She'd also have bet that no matter how he felt about amateur stage productions, he'd have managed to make it home in time if *Faye* had been Amy's houseguest.

After the feasting was over, Evelina gave her speech about what she hoped to do and how the money taken in on the night of the performance would go into the town's treasury. Then she handed out scripts and explained about rehearsals.

The first three would be at the Tully T. Two or three more would be at the Tivoli in town. The professional dancers, including the hero and heroine of the piece, would drive up for these, to get the cast used to working with them. No scripts would be used.

The last would be a full dress rehearsal on the Saturday afternoon before the night of the actual performance. Cast members and understudies would have to be at the theater at least two hours before curtain.

"A run-through in costume helps take the edge off jitters," Evelina told them.

Calvin had grudgingly given Noreen the afternoon off. She made everyone laugh with her exaggerated hip-swinging walk and easily won the part of the "fancy lady with heart of gold." Amy got the part she wanted, too, and despite her size and robust appearance wasn't bad at all.

The dastardly outlaw leader Evelina finally selected was a fellow in his mid-twenties. He had a narrow face, bushy dark hair and a skimpy mustache, which would have to be embellished with makeup crayon to make him an effective Blackjack Sykes.

Though he appeared brash and cocky when he applied for the part, he turned bashful and didn't project in the read-through. He was popular with the town girls, though, judging by the gaggle of teenagers who sat giggling at his every move and cheering him on. That meant he would be good for selling tickets if nothing else. In any case, he would have to do.

The saloon keeper wasn't completely satisfactory, either. He kept stumbling over his lines, even when he was holding his script. It would be all right, however. She'd learned from experience that when someone made mistakes and had to be prompted audibly from the wings, it added to the merriment.

Thanks to Amy's involvement, so many people wanted to participate that the cast of six children was expanded to eleven. The saloon scene, which called for seven, was changed to make room for fourteen. The stage would be crowded, but with such a show of enthusiasm, what could Evelina do?

"Is there going to be anyone left for an audience?" Noreen asked, laughing.

Not until the last of the stragglers was out of sight did Ryan appear. He had two-by-fours and a roll of copper wire in his pickup, indicating that he'd made a side trip after taking Sissy Fox and her dog to the vet's.

"Perfect timing, son!" Amy hooted. "It's all over."

He sauntered over to the table, rubbing his hands together. "Anything left to eat?"

"Not for anybody who isn't a working part of the troupe." Amy winked at Evelina.

"Is the fellow who takes down the tables and puts 'em away considered part of the working troupe?" Ryan folded his arms across his chest. "If not, you gals better get busy. You have a heap of work ahead of you before nightfall."

"Are you talking blackmail?"

"You got it," he said out of the corner of his mouth, villain-style. "If I don't eat, I don't work."

"So eat." Amy threw up her hands in defeat. "I want to get all this cleared away."

Balancing several packages of hot-dog and hamburger buns on one arm, she gathered up the mustard and relish containers and headed for the house.

Tires crunched in the driveway and a car door slammed. Ryan raised a hand in greeting. "It appears Calvin closed early. Good. He can give me a hand with the chairs."

"Excuse me." Evelina reached past him to get a plastic trash bag.

"Found yourself a proper bad man?" Ryan asked, eating potato salad out of the serving dish.

"An excellent one," she lied.

"Then I should be off the hook."

"I didn't know you were on."

"That glare you gave me when I drove in could have turned me to stone."

"I'm just tired." Fastening a dish towel around her waist, she began scooping paper plates and plastic utensils into the bag. "And keyed up at the same time, if that's possible. Nothing excites me like putting one of these shows together."

"Nothing?" Ryan asked slyly as she squeezed past him again. "And I thought maybe I was making you nervous by standing here watching."

"Not while you're eating," she shot back. "When there's food around, ninety-nine percent of your concentration is on it, not me."

His self-satisfied expression said that her denial hadn't convinced him. He was well aware he made her nervous. Her movements were quicker than necessary, and he undoubtedly noticed she was trying to appear busier than she actually was.

Her face, she knew, was flushed, and strands of hair had slipped free of the band. She'd chewed off her lipstick and her mascara had probably smudged under her eyes again.

"So you'd pronounce today a success?" He laid two slices of bread on a cleared section of the table and spread one with mayonnaise and the other with hot mustard.

"I would. Excuse me." As she darted around him, the trash bag she was carrying caught on a corner of the table. It ripped, depositing watermelon rind and unappetizing chunks of other things all over the grass.

"Is there any way you can blame that little accident on me?" he asked drolly. "If there is, you'll find it."

Deciding not to answer, she stooped and began the tedious cleanup.

He put down his sandwich and squatted beside her. "Let me get this."

"I can do it."

"You're the director here. Isn't it beneath your dignity?"

"Not funny."

His eyes pinned hers in a way that told her he was running short of patience. "Change your clothes, Evvie, and we'll take a walk. It'll sweeten your mood."

When she pinned his eyes in return, she almost believed he could read what she was thinking. She wanted to go with him. "I have to help Amy."

"I believe Ma would appreciate our going," he muttered under his breath, shouldering Evelina aside as he went to work. "Not to mention Calvin."

Calvin's shirttail was out. His hair was in need of combing again—or maybe still. He was mopping at his blood-red face with a bandanna and complaining about ocean currents that were altering the weather.

"The lovebirds want to be alone?" she asked with a generous helping of sarcasm. "I can see he took a lot of time spiffing up to come over here."

"Go."

She was about to say no, when she looked down and saw the sticky watermelon stain on her skirt. "How did that happen?"

"Go," he repeated, flicking his fingers at her. "When you get back, I'll show you some of the more interesting sites hereabouts."

"Such as?"

Scooping the last of the litter into the bag, he stood up and tied the top securely. "Such as the school I attended."

She looked properly impressed. "Is there an historical marker?"

"I'm working on it. Get hopping now before I change my mind."

He was right. Walking did help to melt away her tensions. Within half an hour, they had lost sight of the ranch, the woods and the road. The lane they traveled curved around and became a ravine, cutting downward abruptly to end at a brook so clear Evelina could see the bed of smooth stones beneath the surface.

A burst of southwest wind ruffled her hair and brought with it the stirring rangeland scent of sage and mesquite. Evelina inhaled deeply.

Ryan offered her a hand as they leapt across the water to the opposite bank. "Nothing quite like that smell, is there? Better watch. It's habit-forming."

"I can imagine," she said, thinking that his comment could apply to the company, as well.

Up they climbed again through the brush to more shaggy meadow, which rolled toward the foothills. Between stood a huge metal building that looked like an old airplane hangar. A rusty pickup chugged up beside them. The back was a garage sale on wheels. In its battered depths was a snarl of rope, picks, shovels, sleeping bags and canned goods. There was even an ice chest and a rifle.

"Seen the south line?" the driver called to Ryan. "'Bout a mile o' joint post needs sinkin'."

Ryan nodded. "We'll get on it."

"Make it right soon. You're runnin' a lot of heifers."

Dipping his head in a hello to Evelina, the man angled his truck off the path. At the sound of his horn, a scattering of cows moved lazily from the shade of a live oak to get whatever treats he was scattering for them along his way.

Their destination—the school—was a brick, one-story building. In back were slides and swings on a square of gravel. In front was a flagpole and a huge weeping willow.

Sitting in its shade, they watched without speaking as purple began to streak the orange sky. A mockingbird was warming up for his next performance in the upper branches of a chinaberry tree across the road. Beyond were more grasslands, as far as the eye could see.

Ryan leaned back on his elbows. He was wearing an ordinary white shirt, which displayed his tan beautifully. His face was damp from their walk, and his dark hair hung disheveled over his forehead, giving him a rough-and-tumble look Evelina found enormously appealing.

She felt red-faced and dripping. Her mouth was dry. Surely there was a drinking fountain somewhere, unless it had been shut off for the summer. She glanced around, scolding herself for being so hypersensitive to everything about this man.

He was human, after all—flesh, blood, muscles. Muscles. Yes, definitely human, but more particularly, a man. She realized she'd only been giving herself an excuse to take a mind-boggling excursion of his trim, hard-honed body. A heck of a way to control her reactions to him, she thought wryly.

Usually a warning bell went off inside her brain, reminding her that such a man was so spoiled by the attentions of women he accepted adulation as his due. Her best course of action was to stay away from him.

Far away. Her reaction to merely being seated beside this sexy, attractive man was disproportionate. She had no intention of getting involved with him. Not that he was interested in involvement with her. When the hassle of the show was over, she'd never see him again, unless they ran into each other when she came down to see Faye. There wasn't any future in it.

He'd kissed her and he'd practiced his charm on her, but it was only because she was there—like Mount Everest. With some men, that was the same as an engraved invitation.

"I suppose you were big in school sports," she said, wanting to bring his thoughts front and center where she could guard against them.

"Nope." He brushed something off her shoulder and she tensed. "I had to take a job after school. There wasn't time for playing ball."

"I see." If his father had died while he was still a teenager, the ranch, as well as an outside job, would have put a heavy load of responsibility on his shoulders.

"Tell me," he drawled, thrusting out his sensuous lower lip speculatively, "how do those dance classes of yours carry on, while you're here putting Fortune on the map?"

"I don't teach summer school. And I have an aide at the community center who's taking over."

He leaned over and pressed his lips to her shoulder. The resulting warmth created a clear picture in her mind of her neck turning pink, then rose, deepening in hue until it reached her cheeks, where it was now bursting into flame.

She gasped at the unexpected jolt of sensation. Then, talking faster than she normally did, she told about her longtime love of dancing and about her favorite professor who had lent her books about the psychological, as well as physical, benefits of dancing. He suggested that she take courses in psychology and sociology so that she could use her ability to help troubled people— children, in particular.

"So the dance I teach at the center is really dance therapy. It's so new that most community budgets don't allow for it. That's why it's all volunteer."

"But it works?"

"Results have been much better than anyone ever anticipated. People who aren't able to express themselves in words can often communicate with movements, you see."

"How about people with two left feet?"

"Anybody. In the early stages, some students just swing their arms to a slow rhythm while sitting in a chair. We increase the speed of the music gradually until they feel comfortable getting on their feet and dancing to rock music."

"It must be satisfying when that happens."

"It is."

"Do you ever wear your hair down?" Ryan took the weight of her ponytail in his hand and leaned down to nuzzle it.

She silently counted to five, wanting her voice to be steady before she answered. "Rarely," she said, not adding that wearing it up made her feel taller and more sophisticated.

He kissed the warm moist place on her neck where the ponytail had lain. She snapped off a dandelion and brought it to her nose—then pulled it away quickly, remembering the childhood superstition about it glowing yellow on the skin if the person beside you was your true love. There was no sense advertising—just in case.

"I prefer my hair out of the way, when I..." She couldn't remember the rest of her thought.

He edged closer and ran the tip of his finger along her jawline. Her lower lip trembled in unwilling response. The finger continued, tracing the tingling swell of that lip, pulling it down slightly and entering, to edge her teeth.

Her heart soared inside her like a spaceship that couldn't hold still for the countdown. Teeth? How could her teeth being touched create such havoc?

"You can't have it flying every which way when you're executing all those pliés."

It? Oh, yes, they'd been discussing her hair. She smiled drunkenly. "Pliés don't make your hair fly."

"Leaps, then."

The words, formed as his mouth moved along the side of her neck and down, acted as a torch, setting flame to everything in its wake. She squeezed her eyes shut as the movement stopped. He was hindered, fortunately or unfortunately, depending on which side she took with her seesawing emotions, by the buttons at the front of her blouse.

"Any man in particular in your life?" He shifted his weight, and his thigh pressed hers. It was a heated distraction that was turning her to liquid.

"No." Her voice was barely audible. "Not at the moment."

His hands discovered her shoulders, then crept down her arms and up again—testing, memorizing. "Your skin is smooth."

"Thank you," she murmured automatically. She couldn't return the compliment. The palms of his hands were rough.

She wasn't complaining. The sandpapery texture was deliciously exhilarating.

"You're welcome."

His dark eyes, full of warm lights in the dying sun, were an inescapable deterrent to logical thinking. They bored deeper and deeper into hers with each passing second until she felt he was peeling away layer after layer to the person she had never revealed to anyone.

"Was your sister here today?" he asked suddenly.

"No. She wasn't feeling well."

He smoothed her hair back from her forehead, then allowed his fingers to dance through the silky strands before enforcing his implied possession by cupping the back of her head. Leaning toward her, he lowered her to a reclining position. "Nothing serious, I hope."

"No. She's just not used to the heat."

Evelina had barely gotten the words out before his lips went to work on hers, tasting and searching, leaving nothing as it had been when he began.

Something electric streaked through her, and she felt a tiny surge of triumph as she realized that he was changing, as well.

Wanting to know the full impact of this newfound power, she slid her arms around him as if he might be the one who would try to escape. There was a vastness in what was happening between them. Two people satisfying hunger in each other and creating a new hunger at the same time.

Her heart palpitated wildly, as if seeking a new rhythm. For the first time in a very long time, she felt completely, unreservedly happy.

Bending down again, he delivered a feathery kiss to each corner of the mouth he surely realized was ready to accept more—much more. But then, seeming to think better of it, he lay down beside her, shifting his arm to make a pillow of its muscled length for her.

As they gazed through the willow branches, he talked about windmills and how the sound of their working had stirred him as a boy. He spoke of chores that had to be done in the next few days, not only for the Tulley T Ranch, but for surrounding ones. During the summer, most ranchers traded workers.

He talked about sections of fence that needed mending, and she thought of how he looked with his forehead wrinkled in concentration. He talked about how a single cow could consume more than twenty gallons of water on a hot day, and she thought of how his muscles moved beneath his shirt. He talked about cutting alfalfa, and she thought of the heat of his lips, the faint scratch of his mustache and the way she'd trembled in response.

"How old were you when your father died?" she asked quietly.

He sucked in his breath and brought a hand to his chest as though someone had dropped a rock there and it was weighing on him heavily.

"What makes you think he's dead?"

There was a ten-beat pause. "I assumed—"

"You assumed wrong," he said brusquely. "He's alive and kicking. In Minnesota, maybe, this week. Or North Dakota. Who knows? He walked out when I was fifteen."

"How terrible for you. How terrible for Amy."

"Yes. Well..." Ryan's attempt at a laugh was more of a snarl. "Ma thinks he'll see the error of his ways and come back. After all these years, she'd actually let him in the house. It's why she won't give poor Calvin a tumble. She's waiting. And waiting. And waiting."

Two boys were playing catch in the road now. The ball made a thunk, then another and another as it hit each glove in turn.

Ryan rolled to his feet, brushed off his knees and offered her a hand up. "Ready?"

"Ready."

Their eyes collided only briefly. There was no long, lingering look. Their hands were clasped for only a couple of seconds.

Whatever had happened, whatever had almost happened, it was over.

When they returned to the ranch, Amy and Calvin were on the porch. She was sewing. He had fallen asleep in the rocking chair. So much for Ryan's idea of leaving the lovebirds alone.

Later as she dressed for bed, Evelina could hear Ryan moving around in the room next to hers. He was restless, too. Was he thinking of her? No. More likely he was wondering if the problem with an ailing windmill was in the pipe or the cylinder.

She heard the window scrape open. Then she heard something drop onto the floor. A book? His shoe? At last she heard him settle on the bed. The walls must have been very thin. Was he listening to what went on in her room? Guessing what she might be doing? Not likely. Why should he care?

With a sigh she got into bed and covered herself only with a sheet, for the night was warm. Then she picked up the book of poetry Amy had shown her. "To my only love, Amy," it said on the dedication page. She opened it to the first poem and read:

The way was tangled, deep with mire.
The shadowed ever-night was swirling thick
With phantasms of regret.
Yet I stood tall.
For there was Amy. My Amy.

No soul could soar the joyless chasm
Clawed out to snare the terror-filled who tired,
And fell captive to their grim tomorrows.
Yet I smiled.
For there was Amy. My Amy.

Fourteen verses, covering three pages, made up the would-be poet's dubious tribute. The rest of his efforts were no better. It was unfathomable how a sensible woman like Amy could continue to carry a torch for such a man. Not because his poetry was abominable or because his ego must have been gigantic for him to put out good money to have his deathless verse put on paper. Rather because he was a phony and had lived a lie.

Had he fallen captive to his grim tomorrows? If he had, he deserved it.

CHAPTER SIX

THE YELLOW DRIVE FRIENDLY sign on the road to Kurt and Faye's ranch had been peppered with BB-gun pellets. The way was narrow and fenced on both sides.

More parched-looking here than it was closer to town, the powdery land gave off a white glare. Deep cracks, like those that might have been made by a giant prehistoric bird, networked the dry washes. Sycamore and elm gave way to tesajillo, Indian paintbrush and prickly pear, making the hot sun seem even hotter.

As Evelina approached, the stark white house, partially shaded by a handsome cypress, looked like an oasis in the desert. Its outbuildings, including a big red barn, formed a horseshoe around the main living quarters.

Faye was sitting on a porch glider and didn't get up as her sister pulled in and stopped. Her hair was drawn into a topknot of dark ringlets. She wore a silky white blouse with a dipping neckline and push-up sleeves. Her tulip-shaped earrings swung back and forth as she raised a hand in greeting and managed a brave little smile.

"You look wonderful," Evelina said, trying not to make her observation sound like an accusation. With all Faye's complaints about being sick from the heat, she expected her sister to look like Garbo in the final scene of *Camille*.

"Looking and feeling are two different things," Faye muttered. "Don't bother with your luggage. Kurt can bring it in later."

"Where is he?"

"Where he always is, when he isn't out rounding up a steer that's wandered into somebody else's pasture or worrying over a cow with pink eye. He's trying to tame the craziest horse I've ever seen. He's at it all day, every day."

"I guess that goes with the territory."

"I guess it does." Faye's mouth pulled down at the corners. "Help yourself to some lemonade out of the fridge, if you like. If I move, I'll lose my lunch."

"No, thanks. I had ice water at a service station where I stopped for directions."

Somebody shouted, and Evelina looked toward the corral. Two cowboys, complete with wide-brimmed hats, were watching as a third gamely attempted to stay on the back of a horse that didn't think much of the idea. Neighing, it shook its head, then raised on its hind legs.

"Is that Kurt?" she marveled, as the rider pulled back on the reins.

"Sometimes I wonder."

He looked different in his low-slung jeans. He looked so different, in fact, that Evelina might have passed him on the street without turning her head.

"Clang that iron thing." Faye pointed to a triangle of metal that hung from one of the porch braces. "That'll bring him running."

"I don't think he'd appreciate it at the moment." Evelina wasn't quite prepared either for the discomfort of a face-to-face meeting with him after all these months. "He looks busy."

"He's always busy. Unless he's sleeping in front of the TV."

This, Evelina didn't need. Had she arrived just in time to become embroiled in a marital spat? "I think I will have that lemonade," she said. "Then we can talk about how we're going to structure the celebration."

"I'll have one, too," Faye called as the screen door slapped. "Put lots of ice in mine."

The house was an old one with creaky floors. But the rooms were spacious. The furniture was Early American, with lots of maple. The walls, even those in the kitchen, were paneled with knotty pine. The stove and refrigerator were new deluxe models, and the sink was stainless steel.

The vinyl floor needed a good sweeping, though. Fingerprints decorated the switchplate and the refrigerator door. Numerous spills marked the stainless-steel top of the range. The breakfast dishes hadn't been washed, and two pans filled with soapy water sat on the drainboard.

By the time Evelina had washed the glasses for their lemonade, filled them and set them on a tray, Faye had moved into the living room and was stretched out on the sofa.

"It's cooler in here," she said, reaching for her lemonade. "Did you cast all the parts?"

Evelina tried to muster enthusiasm as she recited the details of the previous day. "I wish you'd been there."

Faye shoved out her lower lip as she used to when she was six and not getting her way. Her eyes were moist with hurt. "In other words, like everybody else you think I lie around all day because I'm lazy."

"I didn't say that." Immediately filled with guilt, Evelina realized she wasn't being fair. How could she know how her sister felt? "I only meant you might enjoy yourself if you took part in the project."

The sea-blue eyes narrowed to slits, and Evelina knew she'd said the wrong thing again. "If I took part?" Faye said. "Haven't you read the script? Can't you see all the work I did on it? It reflects weeks of research and polishing. Your story was set up mostly for little kids, remember. The story line was trite and meaningless. I gave it pizzazz."

Now it was Evelina's turn to be outraged. The original script represented weeks writing and rewriting. With effort, she maintained a normal breathing pattern and reminded herself that Faye was having a hard time getting used to the heat and the drastic changes in her life. She didn't mean to be insulting or ungrateful.

"Of course I've read it. You did a brilliant job. But—"

"Hey, there, Evelina." Footsteps sounded on the porch, and a shadow fell across the room as Kurt filled the doorway. He strode in, tossed his dove-gray Stetson onto a handy chair and stood grinning at a place past Evelina's left ear. "It was great of you to come."

"I'm glad to be here," she said. It wasn't entirely true. But it wasn't entirely false, either.

His hair was streaked shades lighter than it had been, and he wore it long. His sun-darkened skin was creased around his eyes. Almost as an afterthought, he loped over to press his lips to his wife's forehead. "How you doing, babe? Okay?"

Faye shrugged and looked away. "I'm exactly as I was doing when you left me hours and hours ago."

He scratched his ear. "Sorry I was so long. But nobody ever threw a saddle on that animal before I got him. I couldn't let him slip back. That happens if you miss a workout."

"Why didn't you buy a horse that was already broken?" Faye whined.

"This one's half Arabian and half quarter horse."

"So?"

"So I like him." Kurt's smile was vague.

No one spoke for a moment, and the silence was distinctly uncomfortable. At last Kurt said, "Did Evelina see her room yet?"

"We were waiting for you to carry in her bags."

"Sure thing. I'll do that now." This time his gaze was fixed somewhere over Evelina's head.

"I imagine you two are pretty busy getting ready for your cruise," she remarked, trailing after him out to the porch and down the steps.

"The cruise. Yeah." He opened the car door, slid the suitcases out easily and picked them up, one in each hand. She had to break into a trot to keep up with him, as he loped around the side of the house and through a breezeway, where he stopped in front of a red-painted door and opened it. "We've got an extra bedroom in the main part of the house, besides the one we're fixing up for an office, but the bed's an old one without good springs. Faye thought you'd be more comfortable out here, away from—" He broke off and stood back to let her go in first.

Away from what? Their quarrels? Or was it something else?

The walls were white, the pullout couch was slipcovered in a blue-and-gold print, and a louvered window looked onto a sparse grass lawn and a rock-bordered persimmon tree. The smell of fresh paint hung in the air.

"You shouldn't have gone to so much trouble."

"Why not? It'll be almost like having your own apartment. It's got its own bathroom and kitchenette." He opened the closet door, slamming a hand against it when it stuck. "Lots of room. Let me know if you need extra hangers."

"It's very nice."

"You'll be able to come and go when you want." He yanked the drapery cord and grinned at the closet door. "Got the curtains in Waco. On sale. The rug came from the spare room."

Evelina couldn't stand it anymore. Clearly her broken heart had been the topic of many family discussions. She was being exiled because they all thought it would be too painful for her to see Kurt and Faye together day after day.

"Poor Evelina," she could imagine her mother saying. "She'll have a difficult time at first."

So Kurt was doing as he'd been advised, trying to break her in gently, the way he was breaking in the horse that wasn't yet saddle-trained, and he was uncomfortable with it.

Drawing on her courage, she dropped her purse on the couch and turned to face him. "Kurt, can we please stop tap-dancing around each other?"

He blinked. "I don't know what you're talking about."

"I was upset with you and Faye at first and understandably hurt. But not anymore. I'm happy for you. There are no hard feelings, and it's okay if we still care about each other. We're like sister and brother now."

For the first time since her arrival, his eyes actually touched hers, and his smile turned into the one she remembered.

"You're sure?"

"Do I look as if I'm suffering?" She held out her arms.

"That's what I thought. Hell, I'm no prize." He walked into her hug. "But Faye thought you might be, well, grieving."

"Never mind what Faye thought. And don't worry if she doesn't fit in yet. Just give her time. She will."

"I wish I could believe that. Sometimes I think..." He looked out the window. "I think maybe she's trying to make it hard on me so I'll sell the place and move back to the city."

"Has she said that?"

"Not in so many words. But you know, I didn't drag her here." He leaned forward with his hands on the sill. "I didn't tell her she had to come or else. She was thrilled about the ranch. And it isn't like she's cut off from the world. There's Austin on one hand and Waco on the other. Lotsa other towns in between."

"I know."

"But from day one she acted like visiting royalty and didn't try to fit in. Now she's set up this crazy celebration nobody needs or wants. Makes me look like a blamed fool."

"You'd be surprised at the turnout yesterday."

"Only because of Amy Garrison. Her approval carries a lot of weight. If you hadn't come along—"

A wild clanging of iron against iron silenced him, and his eyebrows pulled together in a frown. "I'm being summoned."

"Give her time," Evelina repeated.

"Right." A grin twitched a corner of his mouth, and she caught a fleeting glimpse of the man she'd once planned to marry. "Let's go—sis."

While Evelina and Faye went over the proposed itinerary for the festivities to come, Kurt straightened the kitchen and threw together a Tex-Mex stew. Besides not being very good, it was hardly a dish to set in front of a woman with a queazy stomach.

Grumbling about his lack of consideration, Faye picked at it. Then she flounced off to bed, while he drove off to a neighboring ranch. Evelina went back to her own quarters to unpack and change into culottes and a cotton shirt.

The picture on her TV was fuzzy, but according to the newspaper lineup taped to the wall, there was nothing of interest on, anyway, except an old musical at ten o'clock.

Darkness descended as quickly as if someone had pulled down a shade. Too keyed-up to stay shut in unfamiliar quarters alone, Evelina went outside. The vanilla scent of clover from the field between the ranch and the approach road was tantalizing, and she began walking aimlessly.

Was it her imagination, or could she draw the sweet night air more deeply into her lungs than she could back home in Houston? Was this the same sky she saw there? Its star-encrusted black seemed majestic, endless, hers alone to enjoy.

Suddenly it didn't belong only to her. A pair of headlights was cutting a path through the darkness, coming closer and closer. Kurt's ranch was only a modest one, but he, like most, hired seasonal workers, who stayed in the bunkhouse. She'd heard a soft drift of conversation from there earlier. This was probably one of the men arriving.

The vehicle, a Jeep, stopped. The door opened and slammed shut. A shadow shifted and became a man. No, not just a man.

Her hands curled into fists that didn't work properly. "Ryan?"

"I didn't mean to spook you." He came toward her.

The sliver of moon that appeared along with him heightened his cheekbones and hollowed his eyes, giving him a gaunt look. Warm feelings rippled through her. Her breathing shallowed, signaling danger and disarming her at the same time.

"How did you find me?"

"I've been out here before, when the place had different owners."

In spite of herself, Evelina had fantasized about Ryan's visiting her just like this. Nearly like it, anyway. As is the way with fantasies, hers had a bit more flair than actuality. His opening speech had been more flowery, sprinkled with a few compliments.

"I'm surprised to see you," she said. Surprised was hardly the word. He'd actually come looking for her. Was he interested, after all? Her heart picked up a dizzying beat.

"I have something for you."

Puzzled, she waited as he approached. His lips were curved in an appealing smile as he dug into his pocket and brought out something that sparkled when it caught the light.

"My charm bracelet." Her fingers went to her wrist.

"Doesn't the prince collect a kiss when he delivers the glass slipper?"

Her heart beat even faster. "Does he?" Willing herself not to signal her greedy anticipation, she stepped forward and put her lips to his cheek, as if she were kissing an elderly aunt.

"You call that a kiss?" He pulled a long face. "Could've had a mite more gratitude in it."

"It's the best I can do at the end of a busy day." She offered him an impish smile. "I knew where I left the bracelet. I could have picked it up at the rehearsal."

"Ma thought you might worry. She asked me to drop it by."

Ma. So his visit was Amy's idea. She might have known. Her feet felt encased in concrete. "That was nice of her—and you. Thank you again."

He didn't move. "There's another reason I'm here."

"Yes?" She waited.

"Now don't get riled up." He touched the toe of his boot to a pebble in the soft earth at his feet.

"What?"

"Blackjack Sykes bailed out."

"Oh, no." She allowed her hands to drop to her sides in defeat. This was all she needed. Sykes, the outlaw lead was the most important character in the play. The man everyone loved to hate. He was always the one she chose first, as she had chosen Ryan. For some reason, if he was right, everything else fell into place. While the man she'd cast wasn't all he should be, she needed him.

"He said he miscalculated the date of the performance. It comes in the middle of his vacation. He'll be somewhere in Idaho."

She gave Ryan a hopeful look. "I don't suppose you've come to volunteer as a replacement."

"You're right. I haven't. But don't fret. Ma'll find somebody."

"I don't want just somebody."

"You can count on Ma."

"I know."

In the past few minutes, the stars had disappeared and the sky had darkened. Now a light drizzle had begun. Evelina looked toward the house. It was time to go in.

"Would you care to take a drive, maybe get something to eat?" Ryan rubbed his big squarish hands together. There was a long scratch on the back of one. "To celebrate?"

"To celebrate? What?"

"Things getting better." He was studying her shoes. They were fashioned like ballet slippers, a style a man of his practicality would detest. Even if they were comfortable, they were bad for the feet. Her hair was slicked back with only a few wisps across her high forehead. Her culottes were comfortable, but hardly flattering. Her blouse was boxy and hid the lines of her figure.

"There's a movie on TV," she said. "I thought I'd watch it. Besides, I doubt that anything's open."

"I know a place. Nothing fancy. But the food's passable. Then we'll come back and watch the movie together."

"You needn't." She frowned. "It's a musical."

"I'm not opposed to musicals. I'm just against anything that brings a lot of outsiders in. Outsiders raising six kinds of Hades. Tossing lighted cigarettes in the dry brush and causing fires. Leaving beer bottles and trash all over the road. Breaking windows. Causing us to call Waco for backup, to help keep the peace."

"What makes you think all that will happen?"

"Past experience," he retorted, grasping her arm to lead her to the Jeep. "Then there's the hands. They get to celebrating too hard, and it's a week before things are

back to normal. Do you have to let somebody know
you're leaving?''

"No." Except for the light on the porch, the house
was dark. Kurt was still out. "Faye went to bed early.''

The restaurant Ryan mentioned, if it could be called
a restaurant, was a truck stop on the main highway. Its
only decor was ketchup bottles and a dartboard. Two
old-timers sat at one table trading tales about the twister
of '70 that swept an eight-mile-wide path through Lub-
bock.

But the ambience was cozy and the sandwiches good.
Feeling relaxed with Ryan in spite of all her previous
self-warnings, Evelina told him about some of her suc-
cesses with students at the community center and about
her parents' dream of seeing the fifty states, working
their way across the country, east to west, in zigzag
progression.

He talked about his college days and jobs he'd held—
tour guide in a brewery, kitchen-tool demonstrator, dog
walker and even a department-store Santa Claus, all
done to finance his education. He talked about the lean
days at the ranch, and the satisfaction of seeing the
place come to life.

Time vanished magically, and before either of them
could believe it, the burly proprietor was apologetically asking them to leave so he could lock up for the
night.

"Guess we're too late for the movie,'' she said when
she opened the door to her apartment and clicked on the
light.

"I'd as soon settle for a TV weather forecast, if that's
okay with you.''

"Fine. I'll make some coffee.''

Fortunately she'd unpacked and put everything away earlier. No flimsy bras or panties decorated the backs of chairs. Ryan looked around as she went into the tiny kitchenette.

He whistled through his teeth. "Who's this?"

She knew before she turned to look that he was talking about the picture of Faye she'd set on the end table.

"That's my sister," she said tightly. "I thought you knew her."

He peered at it more closely. "So it is. I didn't recognize her in that getup. She doesn't resemble you at all."

"No, she doesn't." Did he suppose she hadn't noticed that before?

He replaced the picture and gave Evelina a quizzical look. "What's wrong, Evvie?"

"Not a thing." She lifted her shoulders and let them drop.

"Like hell. You're upset because I remarked on your sister's picture."

She forced a laugh. "That's ridiculous."

"She's a beautiful woman. If you don't want folks to notice, you shouldn't put her picture out in the open."

"Am I supposed to hide it in a drawer?"

He brought the palms of his hands together. "You don't have to hide her picture. But why put out such a glamorous one? It's a pose a movie star might take. And in a handkerchief-size bathing suit, at that."

"Maybe I should display one of her in an old bathrobe and her hair in rollers, instead."

"Hell, yes. If you'd be more comfortable with it."

She put the coffeepot back on the stove and looked pointedly at the clock. "It's very late and I didn't have much sleep last night."

"It was late when you invited me in, too. The hour didn't seem to bother you then."

She raked her fingers through her hair. "Actually I can't remember inviting you."

"Maybe you didn't. Maybe I just pushed my way in."

"Maybe you did."

He looked at the wall as if he wanted to slam one of his fists through it. "I don't need this."

"The door is right behind you."

For a moment, she was sure he would turn on his heel and stalk out. Instead, he moved toward her. "You have a nasty temper, Evvie. But so do I. It'll be okay, I guess, if we don't get riled at the same time."

Instead of building, her anger seeped away. Her eyes stung with tears she worked to control. When he opened his arms, she stepped into them, pressing her face into his shoulder, like a child who needed to be comforted. Except that she wasn't a child.

As her soft ample breasts flattened against him, he shifted his fingers on her back, allowing them to meander at will, exploring with painstaking slowness the delicate tendons.

With a small sigh, she tilted her face to his, and without hesitation he answered, delivering a kiss so heated it seemed to forge their lips together. So hungry it stole her breath and left her clinging to him, unable to move independently.

Vaguely she became aware of a soft tapping somewhere faraway.

"Somebody's at the door," Ryan muttered against her ear.

"Mmm." She closed her eyes as he kissed her again.

"The door," he repeated.

Not yet free of Ryan's spell, Evelina only listened to the knocking at first, not reacting. At last she went over to answer.

"Is everything okay?" Kurt's hat threw his face into shadow. Noticing Ryan, he thrust out a hand. "Garrison. Thank your Ma, will you, for helping with my wife's little project?"

"I will."

Kurt looked at Evelina with serious dark eyes. Pale streaks of dust marred the tan of his cheeks. "I saw your light and was wondering if you could, you know, look in on Faye before you go to bed. I didn't know you had company."

"What's wrong with Faye?" Evelina asked.

He slapped a hand to his neck. "She needs her back rubbed, but she's kinda irked at me. Something or other I did."

"I'll be over in a minute," Evelina promised.

"It might help her sleep." He looked at Ryan again. "Sorry to bother y'all."

Y'all? As she closed the door, Evelina wondered at his use of the colloquialism. This was Kurt? Kurt of the three-piece suit, shiny BMW and beloved jazz record collection? It was remarkable how the land could change people. Would it change her, too, if she stayed long enough?

Had it already changed her?

Ryan was glancing around the room again. Though he worked at not noticing the offending photograph of Faye, his attention had strayed there again. Why wouldn't it? Faye was truly beautiful.

"Well..." he began, as Evelina came toward him. He looked at his watch. "I'm sorry we didn't get to see that movie."

"Another time."

He caught her shoulders, pulled her close and gave her a brief brotherly kiss that wasn't brotherly at all by the time it was over. Releasing her, he walked backward to the door and opened it.

"Thanks again for bringing my bracelet back," she said, not wanting to see him go.

"Don't mention it. Oh!" He smoothed a hand along the slick white enamel of the doorframe. "I almost forgot. There's a cookout Wednesday at the Tri-Circle Ranch. You look like the cookout type. Want to tag along? There'll be barbecue and roasting ears. Hand-cranked ice cream."

What was the cookout type? she wondered. "I'd love to."

"Fine. I'll pick you up at ten-thirty. Wear shorts so I can ogle your legs."

That was fine with her. Her legs were good and she didn't mind showing them off. But if Ryan wore shorts, as well, it would be a toss-up as to which of them was doing the most ogling.

When he was gone she walked over to the table and picked up her sister's picture.

If Faye was available and she was his date, would he tell her she was the cookout type? Evelina didn't think so. Would he take her where there would be noise and people? No. He'd want her all to himself.

This morning at the Tully T, she'd awakened to discover that Ryan had left early without saying goodbye. Amy said something about tree roots that needed grubbing in the new field. Having expected to see him at breakfast, Evelina had taken great pains in getting ready, doing something special with her hair and thinking of clever things to say that would make her stick in his mind so that he'd want to see her again. Her pride had been badly bruised when she discovered it was all for nothing.

Now he'd invited her to spend a whole day with him. It was an actuality fraught with possibilities. She set the picture down and turned away. She was here, and Faye would be gone by Wednesday.

Maybe her fantasies about what would happen between her and Ryan hadn't come true—yet. But this was a good start.

Funny thing about fantasies. As wonderful as they could be, she was willing to bet that even bare of all the trimmings reality would be far more satisfying.

CHAPTER SEVEN

A JEEP ROARED to a stop in front of Evelina's door and honked. But Ryan wasn't in it. The driver, a blond woman of about thirty-five with a single braid down her back, got out, smiled and came forward to offer a firm handshake.

"I'm May Ballwin, from the Tri-Circle. Ryan asked me to fetch you to the doin's. He's gonna be late and there's no sense in you losing out on the fun."

"Is something wrong?" Evelina asked.

"Didn't you hear the rain last night?" The woman looked up at the sky. "It's clear now, but it was somethin' to see."

Last night? Vaguely Evelina remembered a drumming against the windowpanes and distant thunder. But the chaos of Faye and Kurt's departure, their argument over all the luggage Faye was planning to take and the race to the airport to make their flight had taken its toll. This was followed by the first rehearsal for the pageant.

As Amy hadn't yet succeeded in finding a suitable replacement for Blackjack Sykes, Evelina had put in a call to Patrick Hayes in Houston, hoping he could locate someone. So far, she hadn't heard from him. To make matters worse, half the players hadn't learned their parts.

When it was over and she'd finally closed herself in her apartment, then bathed and fallen into bed, her sleep had been a sound one.

"The rain didn't last long," May said, "but there were flash floods and a lot of runoff. A cow and her calf got mired belly-deep at Creekside. My old man sent for Ryan by two-way. They gotta haul the animals out."

"Will they be able to?"

"I hope." May climbed into the Jeep and reached over to unlock the passenger door. "You know how it is. Sometimes, the little ones especially get sucked under. And sometimes they struggle so hard they die of sheer exhaustion."

"How terrible."

"This can be mean country. Sometimes I wonder why I love it so much." May's braid flopped from side to side when she shook her head. "If they'd stay put, they'd be okay. But cows are a lot like humans, I guess. The next pasture looks greener. We're passing nearby that section, if you care for a look-see."

"Please."

The sun was high and bright now, and the air was rapidly climbing from warm to hot. The dry ground seemed to belie the previous night's storm.

As they rode, May explained about the cookout. It had been held every year as long as she could remember and was a combined effort of two rival spreads.

"I brought a T-shirt for you." She nodded toward the back seat. "Put it on. It'll brand you as being on the Tri-Circle side when the games begin."

Not wanting to be a poor sport, Evelina did as she was told, even though it had taken most of the morning to decide what to wear to make the best impression. A scoop-neck knit blouse in a cool lilac had won out, because it was properly casual and still becoming. It hugged her in the right places and emphasized her small waist.

The Tri-Circle T-shirt would have had to take lessons to be so ugly. Mouse gray, it was sizes too big. It hung below the hem of her shorts and made her look as if she was running around in her grandfather's old night-shirt. But if everyone was wearing one, what could she do?

The Jeep coughed in protest as May swerved off the road, changed gears and started up the hill that put them at a forty-five degree angle. It lurched to a stop.

"This is all the farther I can go in this old tank." She pointed. "They're yonder, over the ridge and straight down. Mind you don't get close. You'll booger the animals."

There was so much brush that at first Evelina saw only the man on horseback. A broken tree limb had been laid across the mud-filled gully, obscuring her vision. Then she saw the cow. It had evidently been rescued successfully. Thinking that its baby's bawl meant it was being hurt, the frightened mother was charging her rescuers. A second man was whooping, waving his hat and attempting to drive her off.

A third man—Ryan—was in the ditch fastening a rope around the chest and legs of the bleating, struggling calf. Another rope went from the limb to Ryan's middle to keep him steady. He was working furiously to scoop out enough mud to free the animal, without being dragged under himself.

At a signal, the man on horseback edged back, pulling the rope taut. More shouting, more scooping and another signal. Again the horseman edged back and the rope tightened. Then again, repeatedly. Evelina held her breath.

Plop, the calf was on the bank.

Ryan, so covered with oozing black muck he was unrecognizable, signaled for another rope. The man on horseback made a loop, threw it to him, and Ryan pulled himself, hand over hand, onto solid ground.

A whoop went up all around, joined by a silent one from Evelina.

May came up behind her and touched a hand to her shoulder. "We better skedaddle, Evvie. Naturally the men'll have to go back home and get duded up. If they see us and come to jaw about what they did, they'll never get to the party."

In another ten minutes, strains of "Cotton-Eyed Joe" reached Evelina's ears, and the Jeep was rattling across the cattle-guard at the entrance of the Tri-Circle.

A gigantic field on the north side of a sprawling hacienda had been roped off and decorated with red, white and blue balloons. A contest, with women riding on the shoulders of their male partners, was already in progress. As a couple in red T-shirts with white letters that spelled out Straight Arrow Ranch crossed the finish line, the cheers were deafening.

"New blood!" cried a woman with dozens of tiny corkscrew curls all over her head. She rushed over to Evelina as she got out of the Jeep. "Hurry. We're short one for the sack race."

Though she was praying May would intercede and help her back out of the competition gracefully, May, too, was pulled into the contest.

"It's been a long time since I participated in anything like this," Evelina said, hoping the admission would disqualify her.

"It's like riding a bicycle. You don't forget how."

Though she'd been afraid she'd play poorly and disgrace Ryan, Evelina came in third, which qualified her for the finals.

Then it was a blindfolded spud hunt, followed by a relay spoon race. When the games were over and "bean time" was called, she was only grateful that she hadn't been called on to try the barrel that had been rigged between ropes to simulate riding a bull.

Predictably Ryan arrived in time to eat. Showered, clean-shaven and delectably virile in a green Western shirt, he joined her at the long buffet table. They even sat together and exchanged a few words before interruptions began. Then he was too busy shaking hands and exchanging pleasantries with other guests to pay much attention to her. The talk moved from the morning rescue to the price of beef to casing that was too small to accommodate drilling tools.

Finally Evelina gave up and concentrated on her food.

The fruit punch was icy. The barbecue sauce was the best she'd ever tasted, and in spite of herself, she actually enjoyed the fried okra she'd helped herself to without realizing what it was. She even had the promised home-cranked ice cream whose calories would cost her several hours of aerobics.

It was time to go home before her escort gave her any real attention.

Now she knew what a "cookout type" was. Ryan had picked her for the part as deliberately as she had chosen him for Blackjack Sykes. A cookout type was a good sport. Someone who mixed well with the crowd and didn't require care and feeding. Someone who allowed a busy rancher to be one of the gang to the men who worked for him. She felt a trifle put upon, not to mention sweaty and grimy to his cool and fresh as the party broke up.

Later as he walked her to her door, it didn't look as if she'd even collect a good-night kiss for her trouble. Not that she wanted one under the circumstances. One of the other guests and his girlfriend had needed a ride home, and naturally Ryan had offered. As Evelina lived closest, she was dropped off first.

His Jeep was waiting, its headlights on and its engine running.

"Hey, Ryan," the girl shouted. "Ask her to the victory party Friday night."

Ryan hesitated a trifle too long to make the invitation genuine. "If she wants to go," he called back, then turned to Evelina. "Do you?"

"Please, Evvie," the girl shouted. "You did us proud today. We'd love to have you."

No, I don't want to go, Mr. Garrison, since you didn't even think to do the inviting yourself, her pride advised her to answer.

"Yes. It should be fun," she said, turning a deaf ear to the inner voice.

Next time she'd refuse. First, she'd make him fall hopelessly in love with her. Then, when he was completely addicted to her, she'd make him wait in line—not too long a line, however.

On Friday night, she'd strike him speechless in the new dress she'd buy when she drove into Austin on Return to Good Fortune business. Then she'd make him sit on the couch and cool his heels while she put on the finishing touches.

Again she was giving in to fantasy. When the big night finally came, she was the one who had to wait.

Ryan arrived with apologies and the announcement that he was behind schedule.

She didn't have to be told that. Ready for almost an hour, she'd feared something had happened to him.

"I tried to phone," he explained. "But nobody answered."

Kurt had locked the door to the main house. She'd heard the ringing, but by the time she was able to figure out which was the right key and work it in the lock, nobody was on the line. So it was a legitimate excuse. But that didn't help her mood.

The dance was an indoor-outdoor one, with a six-piece band providing music for the couples who whirled around a sparkling blue swimming pool shaped in three circles, like the ranch's brand. Again there were huge tables of food and a bartender prepared to concoct the most exotic drinks imaginable, though tap beer seemed to be the most popular choice.

No sooner had they arrived than Ryan was approached by a gaunt man in a silver-trimmed Western suit. He pulled Ryan to one side to talk about a younger brother who was coming from Fort Worth later in the summer and would like a job. "The boy's had no experience, mind. But he's got a heap of ambition...."

When at last Ryan found a moment to dance with her, he asked, "Having a good time?"

It was a ridiculous question under the circumstances, and she was tempted to answer truthfully. But mellowed by the dreamy rendition of "I Can't Help Falling in Love with You" and by the snugness of his arms around her at last, she murmured a soft yes.

Colored lanterns cast rainbow reflections on the water and bounced back again to speckle the dancers with a kind of moondust. Ryan looked wonderful tonight.

He was wearing jeans, as were most of the men, but his shirt was a toasty color that matched his hair. As usual, he wore no jewelry other than the watch with the yellowed face and a twisted piece of hammered gold that held his string tie.

"With all that's been happening tonight, I haven't had a chance to—" He got no further. A woman in a white tent dress cut in, wanting him to meet her husband and daughter.

Deciding that if she retired to one of the unoccupied benches on the other side of the pool, Ryan might notice and join her, Evelina made her way through the crush of dancers. The band was playing "Till Then." The sky was a deep blue and the air was perfumed with summer flowers. She couldn't help thinking how romantic the night was.

At least it had the potential for being romantic if she'd had the company of her escort. As it was, she wasn't even allowed the small joy of solitude. Almost at once, she was joined by her host. Once an oil man, Fred Ballwin claimed to have a hundred stories to tell about his days as a wildcatter and proceeded to tell them to her.

Much, much later, when Ryan drove her home, she was at a loss for what to say. She understood that these get-togethers were designed to combine business with pleasure. Still she couldn't say she'd enjoyed herself. The words would have stuck in her throat.

"I'm sorry about tonight," he said as he walked her to her door. So he wasn't entirely insensitive. "It was why I didn't ask you in the first place. But I should have explained that I wouldn't be able to spend much time with you."

He was right about that, anyway. Much time? Apart from half a dance, he hadn't spent any at all. "I understand," she lied.

"May I come in?" He looked over her shoulder to the room beyond, as if he couldn't imagine that he'd get a refusal.

"I don't have anything to drink, and I'm sure you don't want coffee at this hour."

He placed a hand against the doorframe above her head. He smiled and his eyes looked like velvet. "I haven't told you yet how pretty you look."

She swallowed the ache in her throat. No, he hadn't, and maybe that was part of the reason for her feelings of resentment. A large part. A few words wouldn't have cost him much of his precious time.

She'd worn a sheer white cotton dress with gold butterflies embroidered on the bodice. It hugged her waist and bared her shoulders. Sleeked back only at the sides, her just-done hair fell into the same sort of shimmering curls she'd seen in the magazine picture she'd asked the woman at the salon to copy. She'd expected at least a grunt of appreciation for all her trouble.

"It doesn't matter," she said, looking down at her hands.

"I'll make it up to you."

"You needn't."

"May I come in?" he said, as if he hadn't already asked the question. "That offer of coffee sounds good. We can, oh, watch the news. I need to catch a weather report."

A weather report again? The last time he'd suggested that she'd wound up in his arms.

Did he think he only had to give her a kiss or two, make her feet leave the floor and set her heart to hammering again, and all would be well?

She drew a shivering sigh, abandoned her own arguments and stood aside. If he thought that, he was right.

It was startling what a simple smile could do for his already appealing face. It was even more startling what it did to her determination.

She'd been behaving childishly. Translating today and the party in terms of her own life and the way she acted on recital nights—moving as if she was on roller skates, trying to be everywhere at once, attempting to speak with each parent and offering encouraging words to each student—she could have been more understanding.

"You were a hit, Evvie," Ryan pronounced as she set the steaming cup on the coffee table in front of him. "Everyone liked you."

"I met some very nice people." That much was true.

He looked tired, she thought. Of course he was. Such evenings were exhausting. He'd enjoyed himself as little as she had.

The TV was on and the newscaster was talking about trouble in the Middle East. Ryan slid an arm around her absently, and it was strange. The very lack of passion in the move made it all the more passionate somehow.

Shifting his position, he placed a perfunctory kiss on a spot just below her ear, then his gaze fell on the stack of costume patterns, assorted spools of thread and dress lengths of satin and tulle that lay on the coffee table. Inspired by Amy's enthusiasm for sewing, Evelina had bought more than she could afford at a fabric shop in the city.

"A woman of many talents," he muttered. "You're a seamstress, as well as a dancer?"

"Me?" She laughed. "Not at all. The worst grade I ever got in school was when I was supposed to make an apron in sewing class. I had to rip the seams three times before I got it right. The fabric's for Amy."

His eyebrows almost met with the intensity of his scowl. She could feel his body turn taut and alert. "Amy? As in Ma?"

"Didn't she tell you? She's volunteered to sew costumes for me. I told her it would be difficult to manage long-distance, but she was so enthusiastic, I—"

"Costumes for who?"

For whom, she wanted to correct, teasing him. From the look on his face, though, she doubted he would find it amusing. "Some will be for the upcoming program. But I also keep costumes on hand for my students. Most of the mothers either don't have time to sew or don't know how. When we have a recital, or even for everyday practice, it makes things more exciting for—"

"Ma isn't anybody's servant," he broke in so gruffly she supposed at first he was joking.

"She offered."

"A hint here. A hint there."

"It wasn't like that. She asked me if she could do it. She begged, as a matter of fact."

"Tell those lazy stage mothers of yours to get off their tails and make their own kids' costumes. I won't have anybody using Ma. Not even you." He pointed a finger at her.

"I'm not using her."

"She's so damn trusting of everyone. More than that, she's downright gullible."

He got up and began to pace as he talked about the carloads of sewing his mother had done during the lean years without being paid for it because she was handed a sad story about a husband out of work or a child in need of braces. She made beautiful dresses for other women to go dancing in when she was too overworked to go dancing herself.

Once she'd even been lured by a mail-order company and its glowing promises about how much her sewing could make for her at home. She was given a fixed amount for each item she made, and when he worked it out on paper, Ryan made her realize she'd have to work twenty hours a day to earn enough to pay their utility bills. They'd laughed about it together until tears came to her eyes.

He'd known even then that her tears weren't entirely born of mirth. They came from dashed hopes.

"I can still see her sitting in the chair near the window, where the light's good in the late afternoon—stitch, stitch, stitching."

"I'm not using her," Evelina repeated, outraged by his accusation.

"You're damn right you're not. I'll see to it."

"I'm not crazy about your tone, Garrison." She sprang to her feet, hitting the coffee table in the process and sending some of the coffee sloshing into its saucer.

"Good. Then maybe you'll realize how serious I am about this."

"I'm sorry you have to leave so soon. Thank you for a ... an interesting evening."

Muttering under his breath, he stalked to the door and was gone.

CHAPTER EIGHT

As SHE DIPPED one toe in her warm fragrant bath-water, the telephone rang.

"Be there in a minute," she called to it.

At least this time, she wouldn't have to fly to the house. She'd had the sense to plug an extension into her own wall jack. With a sigh of exasperation, she wriggled into her terry-cloth robe, jerked a knot in the sash and sped to the main room without bothering with slippers.

"Hey, pretty one, are you there?" It was Patrick, the professional dancer who was taking the part of the hero in the Return to Good Fortune musical.

"I'm here."

"In the flesh?"

"I was just stepping into my bath."

An insinuating laugh rumbled in her ear. "Give me a minute to work on that picture, will you?"

"What do you want?" She had worked with Patrick many times before. He was reliable and a good friend. She knew him well enough to know that he didn't mean anything by his teasing. But she wasn't in the mood for his affectionate banter. Her tub was exactly the right temperature and she'd just added bubble bath. Besides, she'd been on the phone all morning to area newspapers, to a printer to arrange for posters, to the square-dance caller to verify the dates and to the la-

dies' church group whose members, at Amy's whee-
dling, had volunteered to supply covered dishes as
backup to the food donated by area merchants in exchange for advertising.

"It's eight-thirty," Patrick said.

"That's the time. Now, how about the weather?"

"I got your message about needing somebody to play
the outlaw."

Evelina groaned. She'd almost forgotten. "And?"

"The dude you mentioned might be available for the
date in question, but the offer has to be firm before he
makes a commitment."

"I won't be sure I'll need him until after tomorrow."
Evelina was still hoping Amy would come through with
a suitable cad for tomorrow's rehearsal. Not only would
an extra professional push the budget, he wouldn't be
as well received as a local.

"He has to know now. I said I'd call him back."

"Try and stall him, Patrick. Please." Evelina visu-
alized her tubful of bubbles popping to nothing.

"I'll give it my best shot."

"How's Jill?" she asked, feeling the need to insert a
bit of camaraderie into the conversation before she
hung up. Patrick and his partner were an inseparable
pair.

"She's right here. Making a nuisance of herself as
usual."

"Evelina," Jill piped up from somewhere in the distance, "tell this overbearing bully we don't need to
practice the numbers for this outing. I can do the steps
in my sleep."

"Jill says hi," Patrick interpreted.

"I appreciate what you're doing," Evelina said. "Let
me get back to you tomorrow night at the latest."

"Hokay. Talk to you then, babe."

Back in the bathroom, she'd just hung her robe on the rack when someone knocked on her door. It had to be Mike, the ranch foreman. Following Kurt's instructions to look out for her, he checked on her, it seemed, every couple of hours.

"Yes, Mike?" she called through the door.

"It's not Mike."

Ryan! Reflexively she clenched her hands into fists.

"I have something to say to you."

"Write me a letter."

"I'll make a racket out here. What will your sister think?"

"She's gone."

He knocked again, louder this time. "I want five minutes of your time. You owe me that."

"Why should I owe you anything?"

"I gave you a hearing that first day. Remember?"

She rolled her eyes ceilingward, checked her bathrobe for gaps and opened the door, with chain intact.

"I'm sorry about the things I said to you."

"You should be," she said, not so easily placated. "You know how fond I am of Amy."

"I know. I'm probably oversensitive where she's concerned."

"Probably?"

"After my father left us, she had to take in washing, ironing, sewing. She had to clean other people's houses." He looked over his shoulder. "Let me in, Evelina. I don't want my sad stories to make the old boys in the bunkhouse cry."

"You've already told me about those early days." Evelina combed her fingers through the tumble of her hair. "I'm getting ready to take a bath."

"I'll scrub your back."

"Go home, Ryan." She wasn't angry with him anymore. But their argument had let her stand back and look at the relationship, if indeed it could be called that. It made her remember how much it had hurt when Kurt walked out. How she'd vowed never to be hurt that way again.

It made her realize how much more serious her emotional dependency on Ryan could become. Hardly a moment passed when she didn't think of him.

The way he would thrust out a hand when he was trying to win an argument, then pull back without saying anything at all. The way he'd make fists when he was under pressure, opening and closing his hands to make the blood flow faster. The way he'd slap a hand to the back of his neck when he was frustrated. The earnest way he was looking at her now.

Growing to care more and more for him would leave her destroyed when she lost him.

"I guarantee you'll want to hear what I have to say," Ryan insisted. "Trust me."

She unfastened the chain and allowed him to enter. "Well?" Her tone made it clear this had better be good.

Jamming his hands into his pockets, he rocked back on his heels as if his revelation would be something that hurt him physically. What a performance. He was a better actor than she'd realized.

"I . . . I'll play Blackjack," he blurted.

She stared at him, certain she'd heard him incorrectly. "Are you saying—"

"Yes, dammit."

"Are you sure you want to do this?"

His laugh was hollow. "I'm sure I don't. But I will. Consider it penance."

"I have your word that you won't back out?"

He held up one hand, two fingers up. "Scout's honor."

"You weren't a Boy Scout."

His offer was the ultimate gesture of sacrifice. Tenderness seized her, obliterating all her arguments, as they stood many long moments considering each other, her eyes searching his, his trying to read acceptance in the depths of hers.

And then—how it happened, she couldn't have said—they were holding each other as people do who haven't seen each other for years.

As far back as she could remember, Evelina had dreamed of hearing beautiful words of assurance at a time like this. She supposed such words were as necessary as kisses or caresses. Now she knew there was language of another sort. A silent language that only two people who felt this close could understand.

His breathing was slow and controlled as he buried his face in the glistening fall of her hair and his hands pressed against her back, molding her to him.

He didn't want to be in her play, she knew. He hated the idea. Yet he was going to do it. What declaration could be more profound?

Her blood ran faster. New longings enveloped her. Her lips felt chafed from kisses she hadn't yet received. Her mouth opened in a sigh that was an invitation, and Ryan accepted eagerly. Then his tongue was inside the sweet recess, moving in gentle accompaniment to his lips.

"You taste good," he said, pulling slightly away. He nuzzled her neck. "You smell good. too." He pulled away again. "And then there's your face."

"It's a common everyday face," she said, embarrassed at his scrutiny.

"That's where you're wrong. There's something about this face that's stuck in my mind from the moment you slid out of the car at the gas station. Even when you fastened me with that drop-dead look, I didn't mind—too much."

"I didn't," she protested. "I was hot and tired and my eye was hurting."

"I was charmed by the way you wore your hair piled high in that charming so-what style that made me want to pluck out those hairpins one by one and watch it swirl around your shoulders."

"You didn't seem to be thinking that."

"When I left Calvin's that day, I was bothered so much by the memory of how hurt you'd looked when I refused your offer I was tempted to make a U-turn, screech up in front of the café again, burst in and say, 'Okay, I'm your man. Where's my script?' just to see if I could put a smile on your face."

"I would never have guessed by the way you acted."

"There are a lot of things you wouldn't have guessed." He pressed his lips to her forehead. "Maybe I'm getting in over my head here."

"I hope so," she said, sliding her arms around his neck.

Beneath her robe, her body warmed, making her feel as though she weren't flesh and blood at all, but softened clay, ready to be shaped into whatever Ryan wished her to be.

A car horn sounded.

He groaned. "I have to go."

"You do? Have to go, I mean. Why?"

"I'm on the way to the airfield." He jabbed a thumb over his shoulder. "Business in Dallas. One of the boys is waiting in the car."

"Oh." Her smile died on her face.

"I won't be back in time for your rehearsal. But you've got my word, I'll make the next one."

"Wait," she called, as he went out the door. "You'll need a script to study."

"Ma supplied me with one. I'll call you."

Smiling to herself, Evelina sat in the tub, not caring that the water was tepid and the bubbles flat. Ryan was going away, but he'd be back. Another piece of her real-life fantasy had fallen into place. What more could she want?

The next morning came and went, though, and Ryan didn't call. This rehearsal was better than the last one had been, though it was far from smooth. One of the spectators agreed to read Ryan's part, but the dialogue sounded stiff and unnatural.

It was difficult for Evelina to work up any enthusiasm, even when she was going over the costume patterns with Amy.

The next day came and went, and still no word from Ryan. What could it mean? She'd never felt so alone.

On Friday, troubled by Ryan's silence, she started off for Tully T on the pretext of visiting Amy. Perhaps he had returned and had been too busy to contact her. Or perhaps he'd called when she was out.

As she passed a field cluttered with idle pumps, pity rippled through her at the broken dreams they represented. They made her think of her own disappointments. Changing her mind about the visit, she turned around and went back to the house.

Though Ryan had kissed her passionately, he hadn't said a word about love. Probably because he didn't love her. He'd told her he liked her taste, her smell, her face. He'd murmured these compliments between kisses. But compliments were noncommittal, easily given and just as easily discarded.

Did he regret his impulsive offer to be in her play and now not have the nerve to tell her he wanted out?

Had he been carried away, trying to make up for their quarrel? Did he, as he'd suggested before he left, feel he'd gotten in over his head? Was he now having second thoughts?

That evening, as she was standing by the corral, looking at the horses, remembering and feeling sorry for herself, she heard the phone in the house jangle.

Patrick, she thought. She hadn't called him back as she'd promised. Would it be too late now to get the actor she'd wanted as a replacement?

In her haste to get inside, she slipped and did a Charlie Chaplin fall, giving the leather-faced foreman cause to grin.

"Have a nice trip, Miss Evelina?" he asked, chortling.

Ignoring him, she got up and raced into the apartment. "Hello," she gasped, trying to form an apology the indignant dancer would accept.

"I have a question."

She gripped the receiver with both hands, recognizing Ryan's voice instantly.

"A trivia question?" she managed.

"Not so trivial. And I don't want you to answer now. I want you to think about it and tell me when I see you tomorrow at rehearsal."

He'll be here, she thought. *He'll be here, after all.*
"This sounds serious."

"You'd better sit down."

"I am sitting."

"Then stand up."

"Ryan!"

"How do you feel about getting married?"

Married? She pulled the receiver away from her ear and held it at arm's length. This had to be his idea of a joke. No doubt it had a hilarious punch line.

"Are you talking about . . . about you and me?"

"Who else? I realize we haven't known each other long," he said, "but in this case, I don't think it's necessary."

There was a long silence, except for the distant mechanical sound of a woman's voice calling flight numbers. "Evvie?"

"I'm here." Or was she?

"I have to go. I'm between planes. As I said, I don't want your answer now, anyway. Think about it hard and let me know."

"Ryan—"

"My flight is boarding. I have to go."

She stood with a hand on the telephone long after the dial tone started and stopped. Think about it, Ryan had said. *Think about it?*

She could have answered him at once without reservation.

Why hadn't she? In her enthusiasm she wanted to whirl around the room. To jump on tables and over chairs. She wanted to open the window and shout her answer so that it could be heard all the way to the Dallas airport—if that's where Ryan was.

Yes, yes, yes!

CHAPTER NINE

THE SUN WAS BARELY UP. It was only six-thirty. Far too early to land on Amy's doorstep. But Evelina found it impossible to sleep any longer or even to stay in her room and wait.

A trip to town, she decided, would be a useful distraction.

Calvin's Café was open. It might be a good idea to stop in and have some of the best apple fritters in Texas, as a hand-painted sign in the window declared, some orange juice and a cup of coffee. It would also give her time to relax, something she hadn't done since receiving Ryan's startling phone call.

Noreen's welcome was exuberant. "I'm so fluttery about today I can hardly stand it," she said, sliding into the booth opposite Evelina. "My husband claims I say my lines in my sleep. Aren't our hero and heroine supposed to arrive?"

"They were in a dance contest last night and will probably get a late start," Evelina said. "But they'll be here."

Though it was tempting, she wouldn't tell Noreen her news. It wouldn't be fair to say anything even to Amy, before she gave Ryan her answer and made it official.

Would he want to be engaged for a time to give Amy a chance to get used to the idea—and to allow them to get to know each other better? Or would he, as she did, prefer to be married at once?

"Aren't you gonna see to Evelina's order?" Calvin asked. It was a slow morning, and he'd been sitting at the end of the counter working a crossword puzzle.

"I would," Noreen shot back. "But it's ten minutes before my shift starts."

"Sometimes I wonder who's boss here," he grumbled, putting down his book. Evelina ordered coffee and apple fritters.

"I found the most fantastic purple dress at a yard sale in Jasper," Noreen went on after Calvin had shuffled off to prepare Evelina's order. "It's satin, and real snug across the fanny. What could be more perfect?"

"Your old man'll blow smoke out of his nose if you wear a getup like that," Calvin muttered.

"I already have, and he loves it. I'm real excited about the show—can hardly wait." Noreen reached into her apron pocket and withdrew a lipstick. After removing the cap, she applied the color, a deep orange, without using a mirror. "Amy's more excited than anybody, though. She has to take it easy, of course, with her heart and all. But I don't think the kind of busy that comes with happy things is stressful, do you?"

"Is there something wrong with Amy's heart?" Evelina asked, concerned.

"She had rheumatic fever as a kid and it did some damage. I mean, she isn't an invalid or anything. She just has to watch herself and not get overtired."

"She doesn't eat right," Calvin said.

Noreen winked. "She eats *here* about half the time. Is that a commentary on your cooking, Cal?"

"Humph!"

"I didn't know," Evelina said slowly, disheartened at the news. Amy looked so strong and healthy. She was always on the go. "Now I understand why Ryan's so protective of her."

"He sure is." Noreen leaned closer. "I think that's one reason he's looking around for a wife. Somebody to be there for Amy while he's away. Somebody to, you know, help run the house."

Looking for a wife? Any wife?

Evelina touched her fingers to her forehead, moving them in an erasing motion. "Why should he consider anything so drastic? Why not hire a live-in housekeeper?"

Noreen wrinkled her nose. "It wouldn't be the same. Amy isn't the type to sit back and let somebody wait on her, even if that somebody's getting paid."

"Still . . ."

"A handful of fellows from the Tully T stopped by during spring roundup. They were joking about how much Ryan had changed in the past year. How he kept talking about settling down. About having kids of his own to take over the ranch some day."

Calvin chuckled. "I reckon he's ready for the big plunge right enough."

"Amy even said so. He's done some broad hinting lately, kidding her about how she'd feel being a grandma." Noreen blotted her lipstick on a paper napkin. "She loves children, you know. But after Ryan was born she couldn't have any more. She miscarried twice. He knows she'd be riding high if she had grandbabies crawling around the house."

"He'd hardly leap into marriage just to provide Amy with grandchildren," Evelina said, not wanting to jump to conclusions.

Calvin snickered. "We all gotta go sometime."

Noreen pointed a finger at him. "Except you."

"Yep. Every town needs its salty old bachelor. The lovable one who sits back and passes out sage advice whether people want to hear it or not."

"Ryan's been antimarriage, a real escape artist, up to now," Noreen went on. "But he's looking at thirty-five, after all. And I'm betting he'll pop the question to the first halfway presentable female who crosses his path."

"Came in kind of early today, didn't you?" Calvin asked Evelina, as he set the apple fritters on the table.

Evelina could only look at the plate. "I wanted to beat traffic."

"Traffic." He squinted out the window at the empty street and scratched his chin. "Yep. Sure is a long line of cars making their way to Fortune these days."

"Let's say I came for your apple fritters," she managed.

He snapped his fingers. "Now *there's* a sensible reason for you."

Evelina inhaled deeply. "Has Ryan been seeing anyone here in town?"

"Off and on," Noreen said. "But I imagine he has a beauty queen or two tucked away to keep him warm when he goes on these business trips. Cripes, look at him. Most any girl would leap at the chance to lead him down the aisle. You're probably too busy with your career to notice, but he's quite a catch."

"What's wrong with your coffee, Evvie?" Calvin asked, stacking the used dishes from the next table onto his wheeled cart.

"Nothing."

"How do you know? You haven't taken a sip."

"I decided I didn't need the extra caffeine."

"Caffeine." Noreen stood up and pressed a hand to the small of her back. "I don't believe in it. Like all those vitamin pills that are supposed to have so much good in them. I only believe in what I can see."

"That's why you're such a nervous Nellie." Calvin looked over the reading glasses he'd perched on the end of his nose to work the crossword puzzle.

"Everybody's a nervous Nellie compared to you," she hooted. "You're so laid back it's pitiful."

"Laid back." He chuckled. "I guess that kid brother of yours is home from college, putting words like that in your mouth."

"Heck no. I just watch TV."

A throbbing had begun in Evelina's temples as she tried to remember exactly what Ryan had said when he proposed. She knew one thing. He hadn't mentioned the word "love."

"It'd have to be someone attractive," Noreen said, settling back into their former conversation. "But I think Ryan would shy away from the glamor-girl type. He'd want someone who would be a good wife to a man in his position. But not anybody who'd turn too many heads or try to come on to the president of the Cattlemen's Association."

"The wife type," Evelina said dully. Was that anything like the cookout type?

"Right. Someone who'd keep a light in the window for him. Someone his friends would like. Someone who could entertain and all, take the burden off Amy. You know."

"I know."

Everyone likes you, Ryan had said after the cookout. So that had been a test to see if she fit in.

I deserve more than that, she thought as she took a sip of coffee to placate Calvin.

"Someone docile," Noreen went on. "And she'd have to have brains, without being too brainy."

"Someone with nice wide hips for easy childbearing," Evelina added grimly.

"And nerves of steel, so she can drive a station wagon full of kids without blowing her top." Noreen adjusted her cap. "Time for me to get to work."

"Past time," Calvin grumbled, settling down to his puzzle again.

Wives weren't supposed to be glamorous, Evelina thought. They baked pies and knitted sweaters. They kept the windowpanes gleaming and saw that the draperies were sent out to be cleaned and fan-folded according to the calendar.

It's comfortable being with you, Evvie. Kurt's dubious compliment rang in her ears again. Comfortable. He hadn't said he loved her, either.

And why should he have? He hadn't.

She'd worn a new blouse today. An overpriced one she'd bought in a moment of weakness, partly because it *was* an extravagance. A special day called for something special to wear, didn't it? Silky soft to the touch—to Ryan's touch—it was a rainbow of colors to offer competition to Amy's beds of brilliant summer flowers. Colors to celebrate the joy in her heart.

Black would have been more suitable.

"You're quiet," Noreen told her, coming back to the table again after passing out menus to three truckers who'd just come in. She adjusted the narrow slats of the blinds against the sun. "The creative process at work?"

"Not this early."

Noreen picked up one of the posters Evelina had brought in to show her. She planned to take it to the printer after rehearsal, when she'd checked the spelling. "Golly," said Noreen. "My name in big red letters. It gives me goose bumps. How many of these are you ordering?"

"About fifty."

"What's another word for sorcerer?" Calvin asked.

"Magician?" Noreen asked.

"Nope. It's gotta end in e-r."

"Necromancer?"

Calvin tugged at his ear. "You must have a college education."

"And work here?" She guffawed. "Nah. I'm a closet crossword-puzzle freak."

The bell tinkled over the door again and the elderly couple Evelina had seen the day she arrived came in and took their booth. Noreen went over, handed them menus, gave them ice water and asked a few questions about their grandson, who was evidently in medical school.

Evelina took another sip of coffee. It was impossible for her to muster enthusiasm for the posters or anything else now. Noreen's revelation about Ryan's need for a wife—any wife—had opened a raw wound inside her. Some fantasy. Her time in Fortune now seemed like a surreal nightmare.

She wanted only one thing. To have the rehearsals, the performance, all of it, over and done with as soon as possible. To see the last of Fortune. And of Ryan Garrison.

CHAPTER TEN

"I THOUGHT we'd never get here." Jill, who was playing the musical's heroine, Marigold, swept down the theater aisle, with Patrick trailing behind. Her lavender jersey costume fit her tall slim body like a second skin, and her hair, drawn back into a long ponytail, bounced from one shoulder to the other as she moved.

She jerked her head toward her partner. "Himself took a wrong turn on the expressway. Himself, who said he didn't need to look at a map. It's a miracle we didn't end up in the gulf."

Patrick hooted. "It's a miracle we got here at all with herself jabbering in my ear." He kissed Evelina on the cheek with a loud smack, took the steps onto the stage two at a time, and looked out over the footlights. "This must have been a vaudeville theater in the old days. I can feel the ghosts."

"Ooooo," Jill moaned, in a thin eery voice. "You've been in the sun too long."

Patrick was thirty-two and looked ten years younger. His sun-streaked light brown hair fell into little-boy curls all over his head. His blue eyes were heavily fringed with lashes much darker than would ordinarily be found on someone so fair. He was Ryan's counterpart. The perfect hero.

He wore a form-fitting gray shirt in a shiny stretch material and darker gray slacks so trim they showed every muscle of his dancer's body. He had a dozen outfits exactly like this one, all in different colors.

He and Jill stood together, complements of each other, and not surprisingly, when Evelina introduced them to the other members of the cast, murmurs of approval traveled around the circle of chairs.

"Where's my archenemy?" Patrick wanted to know. He danced about like a fencer with an invisible sword, showing off for the female members of the troupe. "Blackjack Sykes?"

"Good question." Evelina cast an inquiring look at Amy. "Did he get an attack of cold feet?"

Amy extended her hands out to either side, palms up. "I don't know. He had to ride over to Sissy's place to help flush a cow out of the bear grass. But he should have been back long ago."

"We'll have to start without him." Evelina shaded her eyes with one hand, studied the faces of the spectators and pointed. "You, sir. Would you mind standing in?" She nodded, as the man of her choice touched a finger to his chest. "Yes, you. Please."

"What if this guy doesn't show the night of the performance?" Patrick asked.

"I don't like it at all," Jill added, studying her nails. "I'm getting bad vibes."

"Shall we start?" Evelina called. "We only have the theater for three hours and can't afford to run over. They'll want to start the movie."

After going through entrances and exits with each cast member, she sat on the sidelines, pencil in hand, ready to make notes of all the weak spots—and there were many. Feeling uncharacteristically snappish, she had to clutch her pencil hard to keep from overcorrecting and hurting people's feelings. These weren't professionals, after all. They were doing it for fun.

On the first run-through, they went almost half an hour overtime. Ryan still hadn't arrived.

"We'll have to pick up our pace." She worked for a breezy tone. "Noreen, try your first speech from where you're standing. Don't cross in front of the bar. It'll give us some time."

"Isn't it more dramatic the other way?"

"Let's just see, shall we? And Jill, cut the part about flowers blooming, birds singing and so on. Jump to the main speech."

"If you say so."

One of the biggest problems was the saloon keeper. He spoke too slowly, but there was nothing she could do about it without making him nervous. If she cut any of his lines he might forget the others.

Damn Ryan. He was apparently so sure of her he'd decided it didn't matter if he appeared or not.

They were halfway through the second run, when at last he sauntered down the aisle. "Sorry." He showed a lot of white teeth in what he doubtless supposed was a smile that would make his lack of consideration acceptable. "One of the men broke his arm. We got tied up in the emergency room."

Without replying, Evelina turned her back to him and addressed the rest of the cast. "Let's take it from the start, now that our villain has arrived."

Ryan started to say something, then changed his mind and silently took his position. Though the run-through was better this time, it was clear he hadn't studied his script. Obviously puzzled by her attitude toward him, he kept looking at her and missing his cues. Not having been there when the other actors walked through their positions on stage, he constantly stood in the wrong place, getting in the way of the rehearsed actions.

When he fluffed his lines and couldn't think of the right words, he made up his own, causing a titter of appreciation from the females in the cast.

"This isn't ad-lib, Ryan." Evelina slapped her script against the chair arm for emphasis. "If you don't say the words as written, the other actors won't know when to come in."

His mustache twitched. "Sorry."

"One more time."

Again and again she had to stop the action to correct him for one thing or another. Even more irritating was his attitude toward his mistakes. When the others laughed at him, he laughed, too, thoroughly enjoying what could well turn out to be a disaster.

"Ryan, the menace you're supposed to project will only be effective," she explained, with an exaggerated show of patience, "if you play it as if you're completely serious. Not like a little boy showing off."

He glared at her. "Yes, boss," he growled. "Anything you say, boss."

When rehearsal broke up, prompted by the clock, not by the fact that the play was coming together, Evelina was hardly able to choke out her usual encouraging speech, telling the cast not to worry, that all of them were doing beautifully and that everything would be fine.

"Remember, you have only two more run-throughs before dress rehearsal."

"Three more," a saloon woman corrected. "Those of us who can are getting together Wednesday night, too. Just to be sure."

"That's the spirit," Evelina said with a cheerfulness she didn't feel.

Actually the musical numbers were quite good, considering. Ryan was uncomfortable during the scene with Jill when he was singing about his intent to win Marigold away from the hero. But then, so was everyone else. Though she'd been wrong about a number of other things, she'd been right about his voice. It was as good or better than a lot of professionals, and his tones were true. Besides, Jill, experienced at working with amateurs by now, had learned the art of taking over the stage if anyone in her scenes froze. Patrick had the same knack.

As the cast members began to disperse, Evelina withdrew to the rest room to wash her face, comb her hair and try to pull herself together. She'd promised Amy she would spend the night, expecting to have a lot to talk about and plans to make. Would the woman be hurt if she made an excuse and left early?

When she emerged, Ryan was waiting for her with fire in his eyes. "What was all that about out there?"

"I'm sorry you can't take criticism." She tried to breeze past him, but his arm shot out blocking her. "I'm trying to save the show."

"Maybe you should get someone else for the part."

"Is that the idea? Are you trying to do Blackjack so poorly I'll get a replacement?"

He clapped a hand to the back of his head. "Do you hear yourself? You're beginning to sound like a Hollywood director."

She hunched her shoulders forward and back again in her frustration. "This may be an amateur production, but it means a great deal to a lot of people. If you didn't plan to do your best, you shouldn't have offered.''

"I said I'd do it and I will. But I'm not a professional actor.''

"You can say that again," she blurted without thinking.

He tipped his head back and focused his gaze on the ceiling. Then slowly, gradually, his features softened. "I understand, Evvie. We'll chalk it up to artistic temperament." He gave her one of his killer smiles and brought up a hand to caress her cheek.

She flinched at his touch. "Not at all. It's self-defense. I expect the audience to hate Blackjack. But I'd rather they didn't throw tomatoes at us.''

"Isn't it customary with you theater folk to take an actor to one side where no one can hear before you chew him out? I felt like a blamed fool out there.''

She feigned a sympathetic expression. "I didn't know you were so sensitive.''

"Looks can be deceiving.''

"Evidently.''

He squinted, barely holding his temper in check. "How is it you can take ordinary words and make them sound so insulting?''

"It's a gift.''

Someone was playing chopsticks on the piano. Someone else joined in, hitting sour notes along the way.

"I guess all this is because I was late." Ryan's voice was quiet and deep. "I'm sorry.''

"Don't make excuses for me.''

"I have to. To keep from putting you across my knee and blistering your tail.''

"That wouldn't surprise me, either.''

"Just keep it in mind." Eyes like uncreamed coffee searched her amber ones. He exhaled sharply. "How about if we rehearse together, you and I. It might make it easier for me to understand where I'm going wrong."

"Rehearsal is over."

"But as you say, I'm no professional, so maybe I need private lessons." Making a proper leer à la Blackjack Sykes, he put his arms out on either side of her, trapping her against a panel of painted canvas. "Now I have you at my mercy." Angling his head to one side, he tried to bestow the kiss his ego no doubt told him would turn her into a blob of jelly.

"If you'd read your script," she said, ducking under his arm, "you'd know that Blackjack doesn't kiss Marigold."

"What kind of a scoundrel is he?"

"Besides, Jill is still here. Why don't you ask her if she'll practice with you?"

He swiped an arm across his forehead, pretending to be drenched with perspiration from the hard time she was giving him. "This isn't exactly the reception I expected today."

"No?"

"I didn't try to run you over with my car. I didn't threaten to foreclose the mortgage on your old homestead. I didn't kick your dog. I asked you to marry me."

Daggers flew from her eyes to his. "In other words, you decided it was time to bring a bride home to help run the house. Time to populate the ranch with little clones of yourself."

"How's that?"

"Time to present Amy with grandchildren." She looked past him at an elaborate spiderweb that stretched from one side of a scenery frame to the other. The spider was nowhere in sight.

Ryan didn't hesitate. "Is there anything wrong with that? Ma would be beside herself with joy if we gave her a grandchild or two. Would it be a crime?"

She squeezed her eyes shut. So it was true. Deep inside she'd been hoping he would deny it. That he would declare the love he hadn't declared before and swear that the desire to add the patter of little feet to the Garrison house had nothing to do with his proposal.

"Then you admit you asked me to marry you because I was in the right place at the right time?"

"I didn't just say, 'I need a wife,' close my eyes and point."

"Didn't you?"

In the moments of silence that followed, he composed his face into unreadable lines. Was he angry with her? Was he amused? Was he hurt? She couldn't tell. "I'm not denying that to my way of thinking, a lifelong partner is better chosen by the mind than the heart. And I'll admit it's time I got married and started a family."

"It would be good for your image," she said dully. "As one of the good old boys."

"I'd say it would."

"And so you fed all your prospects into a ... a mental computer and I came up lucky?" How could anyone be so coldblooded? Even Kurt hadn't been that insulting when he broke the news about his love for Faye.

"Isn't that what every man does when he chooses a wife?"

"Wouldn't you like to see my teeth before you make a final decision?" She stretched her mouth into a grimace.

"I hope to see every part of you, Evvie."

On the other side of the curtain Jill was laughing, an affected laugh that ran up and down the musical scale. Her laugh was rather like Faye's.

Someone else was striking chords on the piano.

Ryan was so close Evelina could feel the heat of his body. The scent of him was heady. Never had anyone aroused such emotions in her—good and bad at once. Emotions she hadn't known she was capable of feeling.

"Enough of this infernal nonsense," he muttered through his teeth, sensing her dismay.

She took a quick step to the right, but he moved more quickly, cutting her off. With a small cry, she ducked ineffectively under his arm. He caught her easily this time and half dragged her the two yards to a storage closet. Steadying her with one hand, he opened the door, pushed her in and followed, closing them in together. The latch clicked into place.

"That wasn't smart," she said, breathing hard. "We could be trapped in here."

"I don't give a damn." He tried to catch her face between his hands, but she pulled free and worked herself more deeply into the closet.

"What are you doing?" she cried.

"What do you think I'm doing?"

"Behaving like a jackass."

"Behaving like the villain you've taken me to be from the start."

"Goes to show what a good judge of character I am." In frustration, she brought her fists to the wall that was his chest. "Open the door. It's hot in here. I can't breathe."

"I'll give you mouth-to-mouth." Grabbing her shoulders he forced her backwards through a tangle of mops and brooms and scrub buckets. "Let me show you how it's done."

Sucking in her breath, she made a try at avoiding his mouth. She failed. It trapped hers easily and went to work, bathing her lips with heated moistness before his tongue dipped into the sweet recess she'd attempted to deny him.

"No," she whispered, knowing she couldn't hold out much longer. She was suffocating with her own desire.

"I don't understand what's going through your mind." His words ruffled her hair. His shudder caused a tremor to pass through her like a tidal wave. "Make me understand, Evvie."

"Someone might open the door and find us. Jill. Patrick. One of the cast." The force had gone out of her voice and out of her argument.

The battle was over as far as she was concerned. Explaining anything to him when he was holding her this way was impossible. Her reasons for being angry were all in a jumble. She almost hoped he would ignore her pleas and continue. Then she could tell her common-sense self that the decision had been out of her hands.

"You're right," he said gruffly, his decision to surrender arriving at the same moment. Dropping his hands to his sides, he freed her to brush her hair into place and smooth her blouse. He cleared a path with his foot and fumbled with the doorknob. "This isn't the way."

A part of her hoped the door wouldn't open, but it did. A ripple of cool air drifted over her arms and touched the back of her neck.

Apparently not angry with her, as she supposed he'd been when they were shut into the closet together, Ryan put his mouth close to her ear. "This isn't finished, Evvie. We'll continue our conference later."

"Conference?" Even if he was being facetious, under the circumstances she questioned his use of the word.

"The next couple of weeks are going to be hard traveling," he went on. "The day after this shindig of yours is over, buyers will be here from Kansas City. I'd like to get this settled with you so I can make a few sensible business decisions."

Evelina's shoulders sagged. He hadn't admitted defeat at all. He was experienced enough to know that he'd pierced the shell of her outrage and found the soft trembling core of her womanhood.

That was why he'd abandoned the struggle. Why should he force the issue when the outcome had already been decided by his masterful tactics? Another horse trade brought to a successful conclusion.

He just didn't get it. Surely she wasn't the only woman in the world who needed assurances. Words to hold close and to cherish. She had a right to them. Then again, maybe he couldn't help it. Maybe the word "love" wasn't in his vocabulary.

"There's no need for a conference," she said abruptly, fearing she might find herself weakening again. "We don't have anything more to say to each other."

A muscle began to work in his jaw. "How's that again?"

"In other words, thanks, but no thanks."

"Hey, pretty one." Patrick peered around the curtain. "The theater manager's here. He wants the key to this firetrap."

"I'll be there in a minute." With a shallow sigh, she pressed the back of her hand to her cheek. She was perspiring. The short time in the hundred-degree-plus broom closet had taken its toll.

"I didn't interrupt anything, did I?" Mischievously Patrick looked from Ryan to Evelina and back to Ryan again. Evelina knew he'd tease her about this later.

"Not a thing," she said.

Executing a mocking bow that would have done credit to Blackjack, Ryan stood back to allow her to pass.

Later, as she drove back to the Garrison house with Amy beside her, Evelina hardly understood what the woman was saying. Something about costumes and patterns. Something about Calvin, and something else about the possibility of Evelina's taking a houseboat trip on the gulf with her and Ryan when all this was over.

Evelina nodded and shook her head, she hoped in appropriate places, wishing more than ever that she hadn't promised to stay the night at the Garrison ranch. It was going to be difficult.

Had she been foolish? Would she always regret her hasty judgment? Should she have accepted Ryan's proposal of marriage on any terms? Why was she so angry with him? He'd committed no crime. He'd asked her to marry him. Maybe in time, he'd learn to love her.

Darn. She didn't want anyone *learning* to love her. She wanted to hear thunder and see lightning when she was in the arms of her beloved. She wanted fireworks going off in the sky. But not by herself. She wanted the object of her love to feel those things, too. She wanted someone to look at her the way Kurt had looked at Faye on their wedding day. Every woman deserved that. She wouldn't be cheated out of it.

Maybe they'd even be married and later he would meet the someone who made him hear bells. "I can't hurt poor Evvie," she imagined him saying to the woman he truly loved. "She's a good scout and she trusts me. "

It was ludicrous to project. Miserable as she was, she almost laughed at herself. But she didn't want to be "poor Evvie."

The sight of Jill, waiting on the Garrison porch and reminding her of Faye, her black hair lifted by early-evening breezes, her tights clinging to her long beautiful legs, brought Evelina down to earth. She gripped the steering wheel harder.

"I'm accepting Amy's invitation to stay over," Jill said, coming to meet the car. "But I'll have to bunk in with you, if that's okay."

"Fine." Jill's chatter would drive her to distraction, but what else could she say?

Jill clasped her hands behind her back and raised up on her toes, taking a dancer's position in her enthusiasm. "It's marvelous out here. Fresh country air. The sound of crickets at night. Chickens. Ryan says I can gather eggs in the morning. Wish I could take a picture of that to send my mother. She'd never believe it. And there are horses, too. I haven't been on one for years. Ryan says he might take me riding after dinner."

Evelina moved her thumbs against the palms of her hands. Ryan certainly moved fast. "Where's Patrick?"

she asked, wondering how he liked the idea of his partner and Blackjack Sykes spending time together.

Jill shrugged. "Staying at one of the ranches on the other side of town. A couple of local guys suggested they go raise hell tonight. You know Patrick—he was all for it. Though I can't imagine where one would raise hell in this town."

Dinner conversation was lively. With Amy's enthusiasm over the happenings of the day and Jill's successful attempts to get Ryan to talk about himself, Evelina's silence wasn't even noticed.

Then while she and Amy washed the dishes, Ryan and Jill headed for the trail. Would he show Jill the berry bushes and tell her what was said about the sighting of a redbird? Or would he try another of his lines? He probably had a whole stockpile of them he could use interchangeably.

By the time everything was put away, Calvin arrived with some doughnuts he hadn't sold. "They'll get stale if someone doesn't eat 'em," he said, handing the box to Amy. "Just stick 'em in the microwave and they'll taste fresh. Mighty fine with some of your good coffee."

"I'll see what I can do," Amy told him.

While the two were talking over the events of the day, Evelina decided to take a walk. The rutted road was inviting, and she'd prepared herself for an invigorating hike that left her too tired to do anything but shower and fall into bed.

She got no farther than the school yard, though, where she and Ryan had stopped. Settling on the grass, she rested with her chin on her drawn-up knees, the same position she'd taken as a child when she felt hurt and went off to lick her wounds. In the distance, across a meadow, were cows with red bodies and white faces, grazing contentedly. A man in overalls, with a bandanna tied around his head, was forking hay from the back of a truck. Close by, wasps droned hypnotically.

The sky gradually darkened to a deep murky blue. The man was gone. So were the wasps. No children played in the road. The heat of the afternoon still hung in pockets, and the occasional puffs of breeze did little good. She felt terribly alone.

She wasn't alone, though. She hadn't seen or heard Ryan's approach, but she felt his presence before he spoke, and she tensed for the bitter words they would exchange.

"I thought you went riding," she said.

"I'm back."

"What did Jill answer to your proposal of marriage?" she threw at him, averting her eyes, afraid he would be able to see the hurt in them.

He didn't answer. "Ma wondered where you'd gone."

"So Amy sent you," she said wryly.

"She just said, 'Where's Evvie?'"

"As you can see, I'm here." She drove her fingers through the cool grasses and gazed at the rolling hills in the distance. If Ryan was going to stay, she would have to go.

"I can also see you aren't over your tantrum yet," he said quietly.

"Don't talk to me as if I were a six-year-old."

"Then don't act like one."

When she started to get up, he caught her arm to help her, but she tore it out of his grasp. "Leave me alone."

He caught her again and held her this time. "Since the day we met, you've been behaving entirely without reason. I should be grateful you turned me down. Life with you would be one battle after another.''

"You're right about that.''

"We'd end up like your sister and brother-in-law. Him, busting his tail to make her smile. Her, pining away for bright lights, the theater and shopping malls. While Marigold and I were on the trail, I got to realizing.'' His jaw looked very square and his cheekbones stood out boldly under his skin. "That's what it's all about, isn't it? Why didn't you say so?''

"Is that what you think?''

"But dammit, I'm not grateful. I can't get enough of you.'' The savagery of his hold jarred her against him.

"Who are you to judge Faye's marriage? She's—''

"I'll leave room for you to breathe,'' he interrupted, "but not to talk. You were right. There's been enough talk between us, and none of it gets us anywhere.''

The furious kiss he delivered demanded every atom of her concentration. If he could will her to accept a place in his life, he'd do it now.

Helplessly she found herself responding as she always did. In a moment she would be pressing against him, wanting him, no matter what the consequences.

No.

Without thinking, she pulled back and struck him across the face.

With a roar of fury, he lurched away and put distance between them, as if afraid he might do something he would regret.

"Damn you!'' she cried.

"You hit *me,* and *you're* angry?''

"I'm not the violent type.''

"You could have fooled me." He brought a hand to the cheek that had already turned red from the force of her blow.

She stared at him openmouthed, only that moment grasping the reality of what she'd done. Covering her face with her hands, she threw herself past him and began to run.

CHAPTER ELEVEN

FOR THE FIRST TIME in Evelina's memory, she wasn't looking forward to a performance. Some were more trying than others, but each was exciting in its own way.

Ryan hadn't called since their confrontation at the school yard. Though she hadn't expected to hear from him, she tensed every time the phone rang. She raced to the phone, then hesitated a few seconds to prepare herself before she answered.

At the remaining rehearsal, Ryan had been polite but cool, as if nothing had happened between them. He was up on his part and didn't require any further correction. The other members of the cast buzzed around her and she wasn't forced to turn her attention on Ryan. For this she was grateful. Whatever had almost happened between them was forgotten, at least as far as he was concerned. Maybe he'd already begun looking around for a more suitable wife.

Knowing it was for the best didn't make the break any easier or erase the bitter memory of their last meeting. She could hardly believe she'd slapped him. It was entirely unlike her. Yet when she closed her eyes, she could still see the scarlet imprint on his skin.

She'd flown straight to her room that night, with hasty apologies to Amy that she was tired. She'd feigned sleep when Jill came to bed, and the next morning,

dreading to face him, she'd left quickly while Ryan was
out moving some cows into another pasture.

Trying not to think about him, she kept as busy as she
could, and certainly there was plenty to do. Somehow
time passed, and then Faye and Kurt were home.
Though up to the moment of their departure Kurt had
grumbled at length about the "fool theatrical," about
Faye's turning the town upside down and about how
he'd never live it down, he volunteered to collect the
posters, put them in store windows and oversee the
banners that would be stretched across Main Street.

When he drove to Austin with Faye to buy their costumes for the celebration, he even saved Evelina a trip
by stopping at the Sun Bright Company to verify their
offer of kegs of soft drinks in return for having "Donated by..." prominently displayed.

Still it was only the beginning of chores to be checked
off Evelina's list. She had to verify the delivery and
setup of the portable bathrooms to accommodate possible crowds. The ladies' church group had to be con-
sulted about their pots of chili, homemade bread and
bowls of salad. The bonfires had to be discussed with
the fire chief, as well as parking facilities, a first-aid
station and extra security guards, just in case.

On and on.

At last the big day arrived, and miraculously everything was as it should be. Patrick, who got there early,
offered to make the speech to the cast and get everyone
in position for the final dress rehearsal, giving Evelina
the chance to take a look at the front of the theater,
where the manager had promised to remove the lobby
cards after the last show the night before and replace
them with Return to Good Fortune posters. Seeing their

names in glittery letters was part of the fun for the participants.

The manager had come through. Amy had supplied photos of herself and Ryan, and collected photos from Noreen and the saloon keeper, as well as others in the cast who had speaking parts. The pictures weren't professional eight-by-tens and none of the subjects were in costume, but they added a nice touch.

Ryan had already arrived. She spied him through the double glass doors eating a candy bar. He saw her, too, and though she half expected him to glare and turn away, he touched a hand to the shoulder of the man who was talking with him and came outside.

"Just checking in with you, boss. I'm on time." He polished his fingernails on his shirtfront. "In fact, I'm early and I know my lines backward."

"As long as you know them forward, too." She infused good humor into her voice to match his. "Are you nervous?"

"Foolish question." He held out one hand, making it tremble with exaggerated fear. "How about you?"

"Always. Did you know we're sold out? We have been almost from the moment we put up the posters."

"Didn't I tell you that first day what a good idea this celebration was?" he teased.

"I remember. We'd have to get an audience at gunpoint. Quote, unquote."

"Did I say that?"

"You did."

He folded his arms across his chest and assumed a lofty expression. "I suppose you know, given the success of the show, I'll be asking for a raise in salary."

"I'll triple what you're getting now."

"Stardom is a fleeting thing. A man has to—" He did a double take at the posters. "What the . . . ?"

She fought valiantly not to laugh at his astonishment. Amy had evidently furnished the photograph of him without his knowledge.

"What's wrong?"

"Whose idea was that?"

"I'll give you three guesses."

"Who'd have thought Ma would turn into a stage mother after all these years?"

"The price of fame. Lost anonymity."

He walked backward, almost stepping off the curb into the path of a skateboarder. "How did I get roped into this?"

She blew on her fingernails and polished them on her shoulder, as he had done. "Chalk it up to my irresistible charm."

He didn't smile. "I will."

A horn blasted. A fire-engine red convertible full of teenage boys slowed. "Draw, Garrison!" one of them shouted.

When he looked up, the boys made guns out of their index fingers and shot.

"Something tells me my reputation is going to follow me long after the curtain has come down." He ran an index finger around inside his collar. "Think that's the first time I've been shot at this morning?"

"People are going to start asking for your autograph."

"If I sign one, I'll have to sign them all."

"Writer's cramp is an occupational hazard."

"Hi, guys." Patrick burst through the door and held it open for Evelina. Anyone who didn't know him would assume he was already in costume. Not so. He wore a shocking pink shirt, gray slacks that might have been painted on and half a dozen gold chains around his neck. "There's an awkward spot in the second act I'd like to smooth out. My changes wouldn't affect anybody but me and the prima ballerina, so don't start biting your fingernails."

"Isn't it a little late for changes?" Evelina's protest was a token one. Patrick always got his way, probably because he was a born "stager" and knew exactly what he was doing.

"Better late than not at all. Jill doesn't agree with me, but you know the garden scene, where she's crying into her handkerchief?"

"He's way off base!" Jill cried, coming up behind him. "It's worked the way it is now for dozens of performances."

"Afraid of a little improvement, luv?"

"If it isn't broken, don't fix it."

"But why not make it better?" Patrick took Evelina on one arm and Jill on the other. "Judge for yourself, pretty one. Do you mind, Blackjack, old buddy?"

The dress rehearsal went well. Even the saloon keeper knew his lines. Everyone cheered the news that there was standing room only.

"Maybe we should form a theatrical troupe," Noreen gushed, only partly kidding, "and take the show on the road. I'm beginning to think I have greasepaint in my blood."

Halfway through, Faye swept down the aisle wearing an extravagantly bustled, rose-colored frontier costume, complete with pink velvet hat, and drew oohs and aahs from the others. She was the producer, after all, and should put in an appearance, she said. The cruise had performed a miracle cure. She was feeling fine now and intended to take part in the crowd scene.

"I want to surprise Kurt. And I won't have to do anything but stand there and look pretty, will I?"

It was true. She looked stunning, and knew it.

Ryan took a seat in the front row, patiently waiting for his cue, offering a distraction that made it difficult for Evelina to keep her mind on what she was doing. He wore a wide-brimmed hat and a black suit with ruffled shirtfront and cuffs. A large rhinestone studded the tie at his throat, making him look like the dastardly outlaw-gambler who would have been the downfall of many a woman.

Evelina could still visualize him as he'd looked when she'd first seen him, with his sleeves rolled up to show the stirring strength of his arms and the jeans that had showed every line of his hard-muscled legs.

The slap. The sound of it echoed again in her ears.

Were there truly no hard feelings? Could he have forgotten what she had done so easily? She didn't think so. The performances on stage weren't the only ones that would be given that night.

At last it was show time.

People began filling the auditorium early. The theatergoers were eager to see friends and relatives perform, and though the audience was noisy, when the lights dimmed and the music began, a hush fell over the house.

The smallest children opened the show with their medley of songs, which ended with "Deep in the Heart of Texas," and were rewarded with thunderous applause. Next, the older children narrated a brief history, including the origin of the word "Texas" from an

Indian word meaning "friend," while Patrick and Jill interpreted the readings in modern dance.

The first barroom scene followed, with the cattle baron offering the bag of silver to Blackjack who, looking properly devious, broke into his song about how there would be "more where this came from" when he'd successfully run the settlers off their land.

Evelina relaxed immediately. A few off-key notes marred one of the big cast numbers and the sheriff forgot his cue, but Patrick covered for him and got him back on track. Everyone spoke loudly enough to be heard past the footlights, Amy was dramatically pitiful, Noreen was delightfully sexy, and Ryan was hatefully villainous.

The audience cheered Patrick every time he appeared and booed Ryan so often he had to shout to be heard. To top it off, Calvin's banjo fill-ins between the acts provided a spontaneous community sing that delighted everyone.

There were six curtain calls, and when it was over, a messenger in uniform came down the aisle with an armload of red roses, which he handed over the footlights to Amy, who was so touched she couldn't find her voice.

When the receipts had been counted and expenses figured, Evelina was able to present almost two thousand dollars to the mayor. This didn't include, of course, what would be taken in on the rest of the three-day weekend, minus those expenses that would be figured later.

"I'd like to make Return to Good Fortune an annual event," he announced, a suggestion that was greeted with enthusiastic cheers. "Now let's carry on. There's a heap more fun in store for us."

Kurt took Evelina back to the Garrison ranch later. Amy had insisted she stay there again tonight, and Evelina had agreed—for reasons of her own. As he drove, Kurt couldn't seem to stop talking. His face held a kind of glow, that may or may not have come from the beer he'd downed. Grinning, he slapped a hand on the steering wheel. "Ain't my little gal something?"

Ain't? Little gal? Evelina grimaced. "Faye did very well."

"Imagine." He glanced into the back seat, where Faye, exhausted from her appearance, had stretched out and closed her eyes. She was either asleep or pretending to be. "Putting this whole thing together. I mean, she worked wonders, don't you think? I'm so damn proud of her I could bust."

"I imagine you are," Evelina said. *Why did I bother to come down at all?* she wanted to say, but didn't. The sarcasm was wasted on Kurt. Besides, why try to burst his bubble? She wasn't a mean-spirited person.

So this was the end of it, she thought, listening to her brother-in-law with only half an ear. Her mind was on Ryan. She should have realized that a romance that had burst into flame so quickly would burn out just as quickly. But the realization didn't make the pain more bearable.

The rest of the weekend, judging by the enthusiasm of the townspeople and the out-of-town campers and trailers that filled the parking lots, would take care of itself. The list of participants in the contests was filled. She wouldn't be needed anymore.

She'd already packed everything but her overnight case in the trunk of her car. At sunup, she'd be on her way back to Houston to put her life in order.

"Things'll change for Faye after this," Kurt was saying.

"I hope so."

"But you know—" his voice became almost solemn "—you should have put her name in the advertising copy. As coordinator, maybe? But she understands. It was a hectic occasion." His voice turned jubilant again. "You should have seen the other gals gathering around wanting to be part of next year's celebration!"

"I'm glad," Evelina said.

He pulled the truck to a stop in front of the Garrison house and reached across to open the door. "I'd see you inside, but I want to get Faye home."

"It isn't necessary."

"And, sis—" he leaned toward her, ducking his head "—thanks for coming all the way down to give your moral support."

"You're quite welcome." Her moral support?

"Don't be a stranger now."

Smiling wryly, she watched him drive away before letting herself in. Using mental exhaustion as an excuse, she begged off the coffee and bedtime snack Amy offered, gave the woman a hug and went to her room, where she sank onto the window seat and gazed out the window.

Ryan was out at the corral, sitting on the fence. She could see the glow of a cigarette. Was he relieved now that the play was over? Probably.

She could, and maybe should, have spent her last night with her sister. But she had something to say to Ryan alone, and as much as she would have liked to, she couldn't forget it.

The time was now.

Her sundress had a matching jacket she considered donning to cover her bare shoulders and hide the way its neckline dipped low between her breasts. She rejected the idea. The night was warm. Besides, it didn't really matter now what she was wearing.

"I didn't know you smoked," she said as she approached.

"I don't." He didn't look surprised to see her. "That is, I did. But I quit."

"So I see."

A quick dart of light across the sky caught her attention. "A shooting star."

He made no comment. There was an enormity in the silence that fell between them.

She'd rehearsed the words carefully as she brushed her hair in front of the bathroom mirror, wanting to look presentable when she faced him. She'd even said the words aloud to get them just right. Now they had flown. Perhaps she should have written a prepared statement and read it aloud to him, given her predictable reaction to his presence.

"You were right," he said before she had a chance to begin.

"I was? About what?"

"The show made people happy. You did a great job."

"Thank you."

"I have to admit I even enjoyed my part in it. I didn't think I would."

She smiled at his admission. "You were the perfect scoundrel."

"It comes from long practice." The grin he offered was one she couldn't help but return.

His was a strong face. It spoke of the man he was even before he opened his mouth. Each feature taken separately added something to the entirety, making her think of long-ago crushes on rock stars and football heroes.

Again she wondered if she'd been foolish to let him go. Should she have taken him on any terms? Would she always wonder?

"I want to apologize for slapping you." There, she'd said it.

He nodded. "I wondered when you'd get around to it. It isn't your style to avoid unpleasant tasks. I expected a phone call."

"I thought about it."

"Blackjack would have tied you to the railroad tracks for a trick like that."

"He would have been justified. I'm sorry." She stepped up onto the rail and sat beside him. "Amy was wonderful. I'll bet you're proud of her."

"I can't remember ever seeing her so happy."

"Those roses were a lovely touch. Do you know who sent them? The card only said, 'Congratulations for a beautiful performance by a beautiful girl, who'll always be a star.'"

"Ma has an old beau who lives in Waco. He owns a combination nursery-and-flower shop. The flowers were probably from him. He never forgets her birthday or Christmas."

"I suspected the sender might have been you."

"I wish I'd thought of it."

"Was this old beau at the performance?"

"Ma looked for him to thank him, but there was such a mob."

"I know. Wasn't it wonderful?"

Ryan started to take a puff on his cigarette. Instead, he stared at it blankly and tossed it into a trash drum a few feet away. "She almost married the fellow. But Dad came along and that was that."

"How did she meet your father?"

"He was a salesman for a seed company. Broke his ankle stepping off the front porch and my grandmother offered him room and board until he recovered enough to be on his way." Ryan snapped his fingers. "Ma saw him and that was that. Love at first sight, so the story goes."

"Have you seen him since he left?"

"Once."

"How do you feel about him?"

It was a foolish question and kind of snoopy, but she really wanted to know. She was certain more of Ryan's attitude about life was colored by his father's desertion than he realized.

"If you'd asked me that when I was twenty, I could have answered you easily. I hated him."

"And now?"

He shrugged. "The night he left I was working at the stables. He came to tell me goodbye and I was too shocked to say anything. I just listened. Other people got divorced, sure. But my ma and pa? They were sweethearts. Holding hands all the time, kissing, talking about how much they loved each other. Calling each other pet names. You heard about his poetry."

Evelina nodded.

"Anyway, he told me he'd found someone else. Just like that. Someone who made him feel like a king. He was wearing a blue tie, I remember, one Ma had bought for him for his birthday, with a horse hand-painted on it. He kept twisting it. I guess he was nervous.

"'What about Ma?' I asked him. 'You're supposed to love her.' He tilted his head back and looked up at the sky for a long time. Then he said, 'The magic's gone out of it between your ma and me, son.' The magic's gone out of it? As if that explained everything."

When Evelina didn't say anything he went on, "Maybe if their marriage had been based on something besides moonlight and poetry. Maybe if they'd considered sharing and respect, things could have been different."

"I'm sorry," Evelina said softly, wishing she could reach out and close a hand over his to offer comfort.

"When I stopped crying, I told him I'd find him someday and beat the hell out of him."

"You said that you saw him once...."

"Right after college, I took time off and looked him up. The woman he'd left Ma for was long gone, but there was someone else. I guess he was still looking for the 'magic' he'd talked about. He was drinking too much and looked at least fifteen years older than he should have. He kept talking about the 'good old days,' and how great it would be if a man could live his life over. Now we get Christmas cards from him and an occasional postcard. I send him a check every month—for what he put into the ranch while he was here, you might say. But he's still plugging away on those sales routes."

"It's sad," she said.

"Why am I running on about the past?" He grinned apologetically. "Maybe I'm trying to get sympathy out of you."

"It's working."

"I can tell." With a feather-light touch, he brushed a strand of hair from her forehead. "But forget it. I'm spoiling your special evening."

"Not at all." He looked as if he expected her to make a move. How would he react if she did? His smile was a fleeting one.

Her lip gloss was fresh and tasted of strawberries. She'd applied it for the sole purpose of coming out to the corral to see him. She thought of him kissing it off her mouth. She wanted him to. Or did she? Momentary satisfaction, followed by more hurt later.

He patted his pocket, feeling for another cigarette. He didn't have one.

"I should get some sleep," she said hesitantly.

"I suppose you should," he agreed.

"Good night, then. And thank you."

"Thank you? For what?"

"Oh . . . for being the perfect scoundrel. For having Amy for a mother. So many things."

He nodded gravely. "You're welcome." He sounded painfully formal and proper. "Good night, Evelina."

He'd called her Evelina. Not Evvie. They'd told each other good night, she thought, as she walked back to the house. But what they'd really said was goodbye.

Experiencing a sudden chill, she crossed her arms and rubbed them. Then she quickened her pace.

CHAPTER TWELVE

THE PIANO JOINED the violin, and softly, the other instruments came in. Evelina made a sweeping gesture.

"Slowly, pink flowers, slowly. Toes pointed. That's it."

She raised an arm over her head as the music began to swell, brought the other arm to join it, then lowered both to her sides. "Yellow flowers, to the floor. Now blue. Heads down. That's it. Very good."

She moved quickly to the tape player and clicked it off. "That's all for this afternoon. I'll see you Monday. Same time."

"Miss Pettit." A little girl in a blue leotard broke away from the others and came over to stand shyly to one side. "Was I good, too?"

"Yes, you were, Nancy."

"When do I get a solo dance? I've been taking lessons a long time."

A long time? Three weeks? Evelina closed the lid of the cabinet and snapped the lock, taking care not to look over at the girl's mother who stood watching from the doorway.

"Sometimes learning to dance with others, moving when they do, is harder than dancing alone."

"It is?" The girl twisted a strand of sandy hair around one finger.

"Yes, it is. And you've come a long way in the short time since you've joined the class. I'm proud of you."

The girl smiled brightly. "Goodbye, Miss Pettit." She danced away to tell her mother what the teacher had said—something quite different from what the woman had hoped to hear, Evelina was sure.

She made a mental note to speak to the mother alone as soon as she could, and make her understand that pushing her daughter, especially at this point, could undo all the good that had been done.

The community-center receptionist appeared in the doorway. "Telephone, Evelina. It's your mother."

"Evelina?" Mrs. Pettit's voice was as small and breathy as ever, almost like a child's.

Preparing for a long conversation, Evelina switched the receiver to her other ear. This was a call she'd been anticipating since Faye had broken the news she was pregnant. "Mom? Where are you?"

"We're in Chicago. I just talked to Faye and she said you haven't been to see her for weeks."

"That's true. I've been busy, making up for the time I took off."

"I suppose so. But she could use your help now."

"I don't think she needs me. Kurt has hired a woman to help out with the cleaning, and Faye doesn't even show yet. I promised to drive up during Christmas vacation."

Mrs. Pettit was quiet for a long moment. "I don't see why you can't transfer to a school in Austin. You could at least be with your sister on weekends."

"I can't do that, Mother."

Mrs. Pettit made a little mewling sound. "Well, if you can't, you can't. Uh...how are you and—what's his name?—Patrick, getting on? He's such a beautiful young man. A real Adonis."

Evelina could have predicted this comment, too. When her parents had come to Houston to see how she was making out in a strange city by herself, she had introduced them to Patrick and he'd turned on the charm. Mrs. Pettit had been so charmed, in fact, she'd made up her mind that he would make a wonderful son-in-law. He and Evelina had a lot in common, she'd reasoned. He was a dancer, after all.

"He's fine." Evelina sighed. Beating around the bush took time and the call was long-distance. "There isn't anything between Patrick and me, Mom, I told you. I hardly ever see him. Besides, he's in love with his partner, Jill."

"Nonsense. The two quarrel constantly."

"That's true. But bickering's their way."

"It's a very odd way, if you ask me."

"Different people show their love in different ways."

"Your father and I haven't had a quarrel in over twenty-seven years."

That was because her father had a habit of going for a walk whenever he felt himself getting angry. He stayed away until he cooled off, which was why he was still so trim despite his predilection for raiding the refrigerator in the middle of the night.

Through the window of the parents' viewing room Evelina saw the center's coordinating director pointing to his watch. She was supposed to have vacated the studio to make way for an art class.

"I have to run, Mother," she said. "Give my love to Dad, and have fun in Chicago."

The door swung open then, and the art instructor, a girl who didn't look much older than her students, breezed in. Nodding her greeting, she stood back to allow a knot of preteens entrance. There were bumping and scraping sounds as they opened cabinets, took out partially completed drawings and supplies, and set up the folding chairs that had been lined up against the far wall.

Plucking her sweater from the rack, Evelina checked out with the receptionist and followed the green arrows set into the tiles on the corridor floor that led to the street.

She had the rest of the day free, and thoughts of Faye led her to the Tippy Toes Tot Shop two blocks away, where she considered the array of possible gifts in the display window.

"Look at that cunning little dress," a stout matron in a polyester pantsuit said to a very pregnant young woman next to her. "The pink one with the ruffles. I wish you'd let me buy it for you."

The young woman smiled. "It's going to be a boy, Mama. Remember?"

It was an adorable dress, Evelina agreed. But then, the white one was beautiful, too. She would have liked to buy both for Faye. But in her sister's case, it was too soon to determine the baby's sex.

If she wanted to send a gift, Evelina would have to settle for something suitable for a boy or girl, and it would have to be something she could mail. She turned away from the display window, intending to go into the store, and found herself nose to chest with Ryan.

"Whoa." He caught her by shoulders.

"What are you doing here?" she managed, disoriented by his sudden appearance.

"They told me at the community center that you were going shopping, and named a couple of places where you might be."

"Oh." That still didn't explain why he was in Houston. But she didn't press it.

His warm brown eyes twinkled in the midday sun. He wore a tan jacket, a blue shirt open at the collar and boots. If possible, he looked better than she remembered, though she'd hoped it wouldn't be so. She'd read somewhere, about summer romances, that often the object of a woman's affections lost all his appeal when seen out of the surroundings in which they'd met.

No such luck here. Ryan would have sent her fancies into orbit if she'd seen him in a lily pond with a frog on his head.

"How about dinner?"

"I can't."

"The gal at the center said you were finished for the day."

She pressed a hand to her mouth as her program of excuses went blank. Ryan would never understand the real reason—that she was trying to get him out of her system and the best way to do it was cold turkey.

"I have to buy a present for my sister's baby."

His smile showed even white teeth beneath his gleaming mustache. Why had she always disliked mustaches? Now a man's upper lip looked naked to her without one.

"I'll help you."

"What do you know about babies?"

"Enough to know that a set of golf clubs probably isn't the perfect gift," he said grinning. "Afterward we'll go to dinner. I know a great place."

She glanced down at herself. She wore a mid-thigh-length sweater thrown on over her leotard and tights. And her hair was loose for a change, its glossy length falling untamed around her shoulders. Faye always said she looked like a waif from *Oliver Twist* when she wore it this way. Last night before she'd gone to bed, she'd promised herself a trip to the salon for something different. Now she wished she'd kept that promise.

She straightened her shoulders. If this was the last time Ryan would see her, pride dictated that she give him a more memorable version of herself to remember.

Yes, she would go with him. Had there ever been a doubt? Tomorrow she'd start all over again, working to forget him. Judging by the way she felt standing beside him now, she hadn't made much progress anyway.

"How about it?" he pressed.

"Well, I'd have to go home and change first."

"Fine. We'll shop, then go to your place so you can do whatever it is you think you need to do, then go to dinner. I have news to share with you."

"What might that be?"

"Nope." He extended one hand toward her, palm up. "If you want to hear, we'll do this my way."

"Now you have me curious."

"Good. Let's go."

They ended up finding something they agreed on in a nearby department store. A fuzzy, feet-in sleep set, with a bunny cotton tail. For a small service charge, the store handled the mailing. Evelina bought a cute card and scribbled a message.

Then it was on to her apartment, where Ryan waited in the living room while she showered and changed. The decor wouldn't surprise him, she thought. Rose-painted walls, reflecting her rose-painted world, dreamy Degas prints, delicate ceramic ballerinas and a library of videotapes—mostly musicals. Trophies won in dancing contests. A giant stuffed elephant in a tutu.

Still shower-damp, her hair cooperated only when she fashioned it into a sleek twist. Her blouse had a sophisticated look she hoped offset the plain hairstyle and went well with her slightly flared lavender print skirt.

Ryan's choice for dinner was a restaurant downtown with a plain brick exterior and a rustic interior. It was an old-time cattle drive revisited, with wagon wheels, sawdust, lantern light fixtures, open-pit ovens and cooks dressed like those in an old episode of "Wagon Train."

When they'd ordered their meals, Evelina took a sip of her wine, sat back and tried to appear relaxed. "Now will you tell me?"

Ryan reached across the table to brush a thumb across her knuckles in a remembered way that brought an ache to her throat. "Tell you what?"

"Your news," she prompted, withdrawing her fingers as the waiter approached with a tempting array of appetizers that no cook on the range would have taken the trouble to prepare.

"Ah, my news. It's really an invitation." Ryan dipped a curly corn chip into the guacamole and held it out until she opened her mouth to receive it.

It was unexpectedly spicy, and she reached quickly for her ice water to quench the fire.

Ryan grinned. "Too hot for you?"

"No," she protested, "it's delicious. I simply wasn't ready."

"Try one of these, then." He indicated something that looked like a miniature taco, with a red sauce.

"I think I'll pass." She took another drink of ice water. "Tell me about this invitation."

It would probably be about the houseboat trip to the gulf his mother had mentioned. Perhaps Amy had asked him to come and talk to her about it. She hadn't been answering her telephone.

He finished his taco, set his checkered napkin down and sat back in his chair, looking pleased with himself. "It's an invitation to a wedding."

If Evelina hadn't been eating slowly, fearing what exotic spices might have been used in the rest of the tidbits, she would have choked. Either she was hearing things, or Ryan was extremely insensitive. How could he have thought she'd want to come to his wedding—for who else could possibly be getting married? Did he want to rub her nose in it? Never mind that he'd found someone else so quickly.

What was that old saying? Women are like buses. You miss one, you catch the next.

Her mind whirling with these thoughts, she finally asked, edging the pain out of her voice, "When is it to be?"

"October third. Ma wanted it to be on her birthday."

Was his bride a birthday gift for Amy?

"She wanted to call you, but I told her I'd rather break the news myself and crow about it." He indicated the crisp golden potato wedges on her plate. "These are tasty. They use a special seasoning."

He wanted to crow about it?

Evelina's eyes darted back and forth between his. How could he be so cruel? Or did he believe she had refused his marriage proposal because she honestly didn't care to be his wife? That she was too enamored with city life to be at home on the range? Whatever he thought, he seemed to actually expect her to be pleased.

"You'll come, won't you?"

Why on earth should she? "I don't think I can make it."

Carefully she cut into one of the potato chunks with her fork. It was crispy outside but tender inside. If it had a secret seasoning, though, she was beyond tasting it.

Ryan had found someone else. He was going to be married.

"Why can't you make it?" he wanted to know.

"I've already made arrangements to be in Fortune during the Christmas break. My sister is having a baby, you see, and—"

"I know about the baby, remember?" He plucked a tiny tamale from the platter. "So what would keep you from driving down on a weekend? It isn't that far."

She felt anesthetized, as if she'd been drinking something more powerful than white wine. "It must have been a whirlwind courtship."

"If you call twenty years a whirlwind courtship."

Twenty years? It was a childhood sweetheart, then? Someone he'd met in junior high? At least that was better. She didn't want to think he'd just collared someone on the street after she'd refused him.

"I'm happy for you," she said. "But you can't imagine the problems I'd have, arranging and rearranging classes."

"Then you'd better start rearranging."

She picked up her fork and set it down. "Because dance classes are so Mickey Mouse they're so easily brushed aside?"

"No. Because Ma doesn't get married every year."

Her fork clattered to the floor. She started to retrieve it, but realized in time that she'd probably bump heads with the busboy who rushed to their table.

"Your mother? Amy?"

"Yep. I guess the flowers did the trick."

"What flowers?" she asked weakly.

"The roses. The night of the performance. Ma called to thank the fellow at the florist shop, the old beau she figured had sent them. He didn't know anything about any flowers. He didn't even know about the play. He'd been out of the state."

"Then ... then who?"

"Calvin. He not only sent those particular flowers, but others over the years. All with notes, but no signature. Suspecting something, Ma marched over and wrung the truth out of him, along with a marriage proposal."

Evelina brought her hands to her face, so relieved she was tempted to leap across the table and smother him with kisses.

"Amy and Calvin are getting married."

"Isn't that what I've been saying?"

"No. Yes. In a way. I didn't know."

He snapped his fingers in front of her face. "Wake up, Evvie."

"I thought... Oh, of course, I'll be there. I wouldn't dream of missing that wedding." The potatoes were delicious, after all, she decided. And the little tacos weren't too hot. They were perfect.

He waited. "Don't you want to say something to me?"

"About what?"

"About how I was right. Ma and Calvin."

"You were right," she said obediently.

Though the piped-in music was subdued and romantic, it had an insistent rhythm that refused to stay in the background. Her heart began to mimic the throbbing beat as Ryan reached across the table again to take her hand. Something uncommon glistened in the depths of his eyes.

"I was right about something else, too."

Her stomach muscles tightened. "What?"

"About— This is no good," he interrupted himself, signaling for the check.

"You don't like the food, after all?"

"I don't like the crowd." He smiled thinly. "We have too much to talk about."

She stared at her plate. "We shouldn't."

"Why shouldn't we?"

"You and I aren't... aren't compatible."

"We'll talk about it later," he said, leaving enough money on the table to cover the check and tip. "Let's go."

He tucked her into the car, got in himself and turned out of the parking lot. She sat stiffly with her hands in her lap, like a shy little girl going to a tea party at the home of someone she hardly knew.

And then they were in the underground garage of her building. She tensed, preparing to say the words that would send him on his way. She couldn't let him come inside. If she did, all would be lost. But the words didn't emerge.

Now they were at the door. The key clicked in the lock. The knob turned and they were inside. Ryan's fingers tensed at her back, relaxed and tensed again.

The music from the restaurant still throbbed in Evelina's blood, making her think of the woods and the redbird whose sighting was responsible for the warmest, sweetest kisses she'd ever known.

Now his mouth was at her ear, and she stopped struggling with rationality. Now it was at the pulsing hollow of her throat, and she found herself wanting to feel it against her breast. The weight of her lids forced her eyes closed, but she opened them again quickly. He might consider it total surrender.

"Still think we're not compatible?" he asked huskily.

"I... I don't know."

"Maybe I can help you decide," he said, as his lips began to blaze a relentless path to hers.

"Would you like a glass of water?" she asked quickly while she still had a voice.

"A glass of water?" He rested his forehead against hers. "Now?"

"I'm really thirsty."

"You're thirsty." Reluctantly he pulled away. "I'll get it. With ice?"

"Just water will be fine."

"Don't move. I don't want to forget where we left off."

As if she could. A few deep breaths helped a bit. The clinking of glasses and the sound of running water helped a bit more. A horn honked three times in succession in the street below. Someone shouted for someone else to hurry.

Despite what Ryan had said about not moving, she walked onto the balcony. The view wasn't worthy of conversation. The lights came from passing cars, a McDonald's and a movie theater.

There must be something they could talk about that would distract them long enough for common sense to make an appearance. Or did she want to be distracted? Was what she felt for Ryan too big to dismiss?

As he joined her on the balcony, she gave it a try. "The church won't be big enough to hold all Amy's friends," she said.

"The guest list is long. It'll be an occasion to remember all right."

Calvin's friends were throwing him a bachelor party, and Noreen was arranging something similar for Amy. A last-minute bridal shower. Evelina might consider driving down early to be part of it, he suggested, as he handed her a clinking glass—he'd put ice in, after all—with a picture of a dancing mouse on the side.

"Ma would like it if you were there. She's fond of you."

"I'm fond of her, too."

"It's great the way you two hit it off." He waited until she had a sip, then sank onto the chaise longue, drawing her down beside him.

"I know," she agreed, unable to completely quiet the small warning voice inside her. It was always convenient when mother and prospective daughter-in-law were friends.

Was that friendship a prerequisite to the marriage contract? the little voice inside her whispered. Are you and Ryan compatible? Truly compatible?

With increasing desperation, she tried again. Maybe he *did* love her. Didn't his driving all the way to Houston prove it? Didn't his all-possessing kisses mean something? Didn't they?

Overhead was a single gathering of stars, seven of them in a V-shape. One was much larger than the others. A star for wishing.

Star light, star bright . . .

"They'll be very happy together," she said, more to herself than to Ryan. The ice clinked in her glass, reminding her of childhood days when Faye had made fun of her habit of chewing on ice cubes. *If you could see yourself,* Faye used to say, *it makes you look like Bugs Bunny.*

"There aren't any guarantees." Sliding an arm around her, Ryan pressed a kiss into her hair.

"There are in this case. Calvin must love Amy very much."

His laugh rumbled against her ear as he placed another kiss there. "What finally made you come to that conclusion? Because he sent the roses? He's shown his caring in a damn sight more ways than that."

"At least he declared himself. I think it's romantic."

"To my way of thinking, it's sad. Ma wasted a helluva lot of time holding on to a dream."

"But she found a dream that's even better."

"It almost didn't happen."

"But it did."

"By chance."

Chance was another name for destiny. "Destiny," she said aloud, liking the sound of it.

"Destiny." He pretended to shiver. "It's a frightening word."

"Frightening how?"

"It brings up a picture of a man barreling down a steep hill toward something he can't avoid."

"Maybe that's how it should be. If it's something good."

"How can anything happen for the good if it isn't thought out to the last detail? Life is too complicated for anyone to sit back and accept fate."

Everything planned.

Planned the way he planned to marry Evelina because Amy was fond of her? Because he was ready for a wife and children?

Oh, maybe there was more to it. Certainly he was attracted to her. But physical attraction wasn't enough. Not nearly enough. So he'd driven to Houston to see her. He'd probably drive a lot farther to look at a good horse.

His kiss to the shoulder seared her skin through the fabric of her blouse. She stiffened against it. "I admire you," she said.

"I admire you, too." A smile quivered at one corner of his mouth. "Now. Where were we?"

"I admire you because you work out all the details of your life so carefully. Everything has to have a reason for being."

"Why do I get the feeling that isn't a compliment?"

"Why am I here with you?" she persisted.

"Why?" He scowled, pretending that her question was one that required careful thought. "A kiss that feels the way your kiss feels to me, isn't to be taken lightly, Evvie. You've become a habit I can't seem to break."

"Like brushing your teeth and shaving."

"You could put it that way."

"You came here to make love to me, didn't you?" she accused, too mixed-up to focus clearly on what she was trying to say. "Lovemaking could be considered a cure, couldn't it?"

Quizzical surprise flickered over his face. "A cure?"

"You know—a release that leaves you free to get on with the more important things in life."

"Now wait a minute..." His voice took on a sharp edge.

"Like a good back rub."

"What's wrong, Evvie?" He withdrew his arm. "You're with me because you wanted to be with me. I didn't seduce you."

"That's something Blackjack would say."

"Maybe there's a little Blackjack in all of us."

"In some more than others."

He threw up one hand in despair. "I thought we'd come to an understanding."

"Is that what we did?"

"This isn't getting us anywhere."

"And time is money. We mustn't waste any of it."

"As a matter of fact, I put off a hell of a lot of important business to come here—"

"Then you'd better get back to it," she interrupted. Smoothing her skirt, she stood up and went back into the living room, then crossed deliberately to the mirror to check her hair. Her face looked mottled in the gold-flecked glass.

"Is it the dancing that's rattled your senses?" he asked, following her in.

"No. You have. I don't think I can take any more."

"Well, it was fun while it lasted."

"Is that what it was? Fun?"

"Hell, I hope so." He crossed to the door in three long strides and left, without looking back.

A horn sounded from outside the window and she hurried to the open balcony door, half hoping it was Ryan, signaling that it was all a misunderstanding. That he was coming back to talk things over.

It wasn't him, and it was just as well. They had nothing more to say to each other.

CHAPTER THIRTEEN

THERE WERE NO SURPRISES in Fortune. Evelina expected the church to be crowded and it was. She expected Amy to look beautiful and she did. Her wedding dress was peach organza with an overlay of lace. She'd had her hair permed into soft, all-over waves. Though she was seven years older than the groom, she didn't look it.

Evelina had expected Ryan to look handsome and he did. Gone was the working cowboy look. Had he been wearing the beautifully tailored blue suit and satiny tie the day she met him, she never would have chosen him for Blackjack Sykes, and her troubles might never have begun.

When he saw her, he nodded. But he didn't salute as he usually did, and his eyes didn't crinkle.

The reception was held in the church hall. Refreshments were dainty sandwiches, wedding cake and punch. The couple had decided to save the money a large celebration would have cost to invest in a month-long honeymoon. They were going to Nashville, Tennessee, first to visit Opryland, and when Calvin sat down with his banjo to play and sing "Once in Love with Amy," one of his cronies asked if he was going to appear at the Grand Old Opry while he was there.

Evelina had come two days early to look in on Faye and Kurt. That way she would only have to stay in Fortune long enough to wish the couple happiness. She'd start home as soon as the bridal bouquet was thrown—though she'd make a point not to stand anywhere she had a chance of catching it.

Typical of the shortsightedness she'd displayed lately, she'd left her car at the Garrison house and ridden to the church with Noreen. Now she'd have to wait until the woman was ready to leave, and as gregarious as Noreen was, it was anyone's guess when that would be.

While she was waiting, she accepted a dance with the saloon keeper from the musical, who tried to convince her to take over the show again next year, using him in one of the star spots. Then, to show there were no hard feelings, she danced with the young man who'd backed out of the Blackjack role—and even managed a smile when he admitted that he'd lied.

"I wasn't really gonna be out of town," he said. "But when I thought of getting up on that stage with everybody staring at me, I couldn't do it."

Next she had a waltz with Calvin, who looked unlike himself in his new pin-striped suit and with his hair neatly trimmed. To her surprise, he turned out to be a wonderful dancer. He confessed that he'd taken lessons at an Arthur Murray studio a few years before and knew how to tango, rhumba and do the Bunny Hop.

"But if you tell anybody," he said with a deadpan expression that made it hard to know if he was teasing, "I'll deny the whole thing."

When he left her at the edge of the floor and went in search of his bride, Evelina stood on tiptoe to look over the sea of faces for Noreen. There she was, at the punch bowl. Would she want to leave yet?

Fingers curved lightly around her upper arm. "Care to dance?" someone asked close to her ear. It was Ryan.

She wasn't flattered by his invitation, and she certainly wasn't hopeful of a reconciliation. He was the bride's son. Courtesy dictated that he shake hands with all the men and dance with all the women. Courtesy dictated, too, that she accept, and so she did, stepping into his arms without giving verbal acceptance.

How she wished things could have been otherwise. That he was dancing with her because no other woman made him feel the way she did. Because they shared something special. Because... Suddenly tears filled her eyes.

"You're one of those females who cry at weddings," he accused, cocking his head to one side to look more fully into her face.

"Even when they're on TV." She mugged comically, relieved that he'd pounced on a good reason for the tears that glistened in her eyes.

"You look very pretty."

"So do you," she said with a flippancy she didn't feel.

The rest of their exchange was stilted. Though Evelina tried to think of something clever to say, her well of ideas had run dry. She wanted something noncommittal, yet suitable to the occasion. It was like selecting a proper verse on a greeting card from a rack with a very limited selection.

Ryan fared no better. Their last meeting had evidently obviated their easy sense of camaraderie. They danced in virtual silence—a silence far louder than the most animated of conversations.

She was grateful when Amy came from nowhere and pulled them off to the side. "Ryan," she said in a voice that was pitched an octave higher than usual with her excitement, "Sissy is here. Will you give her some attention? The poor thing is all alone. She got a ride to the church from one of her neighbors, but she needs a lift home, if you can manage it."

"I'd be happy to," he said, and he probably *was* happy—to escape. After telling his mother how beautiful she looked, warning her to tell Calvin to drive carefully and giving her a bear hug, he dashed off.

When he was gone, Amy touched a hand to Evelina's shoulder. "Honey, I'm such a scatterbrain. We'll be leaving as soon as I change, and I forgot to bring your package here."

"Package?" Evelina echoed vaguely. Her peripheral vision showed her Ryan, leading a delicate little woman with birdlike features and dyed red hair onto the dance floor.

"The costumes. Don't you remember? They're finished."

"Of course." In the excitement, Evelina had forgotten the sewing Amy had been doing for her. There was a Snow Princess costume and a set of elf outfits. They'd decided that she would take them back with her to save time and mailing charges. "Don't worry about it. I have to go back to the house, anyway, to get my car. You concentrate on being happy."

"That won't take much concentration." Amy gave her a hearty squeeze. "It would be impossible for anyone to be happier than I am at this moment."

"I can tell by looking at you. You're glowing."

"Am I? I was so nervous I almost went down the aisle in bare feet! Oh, honey, I'm so lucky to have him. Calvin's a gruff old codger on the surface, but underneath..." She pressed her fingers to her lips as her voice broke, and she was unable to go on for a few moments. Then she cleared her throat. "Your package is in the sun room. On the daybed. Your name is printed with marking pen. You'll find the key under the geranium pot on the porch."

"No problem. Now forget about it and have a wonderful time."

Half an hour later Evelina was able to capture Noreen, and they were on their way. When the Garrison house loomed into view, she asked Noreen to let her off at the road.

"I don't mind taking you up to the porch."

"No, that's okay."

She could see the Jeep and knew Ryan was already home. The exchanged hugs, goodbyes and car doors slamming would alert him to her presence. Evelina hoped to collect her package and escape before he realized she'd been there.

The light was on in his room, but the rest of the house was in darkness. The key was under the geranium pot as Amy had told her. The door opened without a squeak, and the floor didn't do any telltale creaking. She found her package easily and slipped away, without turning on the lights.

So far, so good. Ryan hadn't heard her.

Or maybe he had. Maybe he was hiding behind his closed door, waiting for her to be gone.

Thrusting aside unpleasant thoughts, she turned the key in the ignition of her car. Nothing. Again. The yellow alternator light came on in the dashboard—whatever that meant.

Groaning to herself, she got out and raised the hood, though she didn't know what she expected to find. If the workings of a washing machine were in the cavern she wouldn't have known the difference. All she got for her trouble was a smear of black grease on her forearm.

As quietly as she could, she retrieved the key and slipped into the house again. The long cord on the telephone allowed her to take the instrument into the sun room and close the door, so she could look up the number of the gas station in the directory and dial.

A woman answered and told her the mechanic had gone to Amy and Calvin's wedding. She didn't expect him back tonight.

"The wedding's been over for hours," Evelina protested.

The woman laughed. "Not for my husband and his brother. They'll use it as an excuse to celebrate the rest of this week."

"Is there someone else I can call?"

"The station on the highway. But not until morning. They're closed, too."

Now what? She could walk to the hotel in town, but that would be foolish. Amy would be upset if she found out. She could call Faye and ask Kurt to come and get her, but they might have gone to bed early, as they had most nights since she became pregnant. Besides, Ryan would discover her car in the morning and wonder about it. He might even think she'd met with foul play and call the sheriff.

She could leave him a note.

No. He might not see it. She had no choice but to knock on his door.

He'd been working at his desk. His hair looked as if he'd combed his fingers through it in the process of thinking. He was still wearing the white shirt from the wedding, but the collar was open and his sleeves were rolled up. He had a smudge of black on his shirtfront. Sissy Fox had evidently put him to work when he'd taken her home.

"Your shirt," she said, indicating the streak with a flutter of one hand. "You should get that off before it sets."

"Did you knock on my door to tell me that?"

"Hardly. I only saw it now." Under his dark gaze she almost forgot why she *had* knocked. "My car won't start. Could you look at it?"

"I'd be happy to." He shrugged. "But it won't do any good. Ranching's *my* game." He brushed at the grimy spot with one hand, making it worse.

She considered asking him to take the shirt off so she could clean it for him, but decided against it. Best to keep this on an impersonal level. He was perfectly capable of seeing to his own wardrobe. "You don't know anything about cars?"

"I know you put gas in them to make them run."

"Super. I thought boys were required to take auto mechanics in high school."

He braced a hand against the doorjamb and smirked. "Aren't you being sexist? Why shouldn't it be a required course for girls, too?"

Deciding not to take part in a debate, she looked over her shoulder in the general direction of her car. "Now what am I going to do?"

"Stay over." His expression said he didn't care what she decided. "The guest room's unoccupied."

"I suppose I have no choice."

"What a gracious acceptance."

"I don't feel very gracious."

One shaggy eyebrow peaked and the other lowered. "You know the way."

"Yes. Thank you." When he started to close the door, she stopped him. "Do you mind if I make some coffee?"

"Give me a call when it's ready. I could use a break. I'm not much good at paperwork."

Seconds later she heard typing, hunt-and-peck style. Coffee? She didn't really want it. Her nerves were jangled enough. Better a glass of milk and some bacon and eggs. Though the table at the reception had been set with everything imaginable to tweak the appetite, she'd eaten almost nothing. Only a sliver of wedding cake. Now she felt hungry.

Should she knock on Ryan's door again and ask if he wanted something to eat, too? No. With his appetite, he'd accept even if the fare was chocolate-covered grasshoppers.

"Ready," she called, putting her mouth close to the crack in his door when she'd thrown a hasty meal together.

"Be right with you."

As she suspected, he was happy to eat. After he finished everything she put in front of him, he asked if there were second helpings. As they ate, he related some of the problems he'd had with an outfit whose ownership had changed recently. She talked about how nervous she was about a quarterly meeting at the center. Dance therapy was still on trial, and she wasn't sure it would be continued.

When Ryan had downed everything in sight, he scraped back his chair with an air of finality and stood. "Thanks, Evvie. That hit the spot."

"Thank *you* for your hospitality."

"I have a few rounds to make in the morning, but if you'd rather, I'll stick around and see if I can find somebody who'll get your car started."

"There's a service station on the highway that'll be open, I was told. A call will bring me all the help I need."

"Suit yourself," he said. "Well…good night, then."

Was it her imagination, she wondered, as she stared at the door he'd very nearly closed in her face, or had she seen relief mirrored in the eyes that barely touched hers?

CHAPTER FOURTEEN

AFTER A SOOTHING BATH in the old-fashioned claw-foot tub, Evelina smoothed on a body lotion that smelled of roses. Minutes later she lay between fresh-scented percale sheets, the orange-and-yellow quilt folded back and the curtains billowing with the whims of a delightful breeze.

The springs creaked when she reached back to fluff her pillow, and again, as she lay down. The same kind of creaking came from the next room—where Ryan was sleeping.

She turned and the springs creaked again. Ryan's bedsprings answered. She smiled to herself. It was their own duet. Not exactly the "Indian Love Call"...

"Ryan?"

"Yep?"

"It was a beautiful wedding, wasn't it?"

"Mmm." His springs creaked again. "Trouble sleeping?"

"A little."

"Seeing Ma get married made you think of that other joker?"

"What other joker?"

"The fellow who makes you draw your guns whenever a man gets too close."

Her heartbeat quickened. Had she told him about Kurt? No. She wouldn't have. He had spoken with Faye at the performance back in August, but her sister wouldn't have touched on that subject in a casual conversation, would she?

But maybe, now that Faye's social life was blooming, their paths had crossed in the weeks since and Faye had. As a reward for the wonderful job she did with Return to Good Fortune, Kurt bought her a little red car so that she could zip into town whenever she felt like it.

"I wasn't thinking about him," Evelina said.

"You were in love with him?"

"I thought I was."

"But you weren't?"

"No." Since Ryan had come into her life, she realized that what she'd felt for Kurt couldn't be called love by the widest stretch of the imagination.

"I bet you told him you were." Even through the walls she could sense his I-told-you-so. "That goes to show how much pretty words can be trusted."

She set her teeth together and released a long breath. "Actions speak louder?"

"Yep."

"Like Calvin doing things for Amy all those years. Being there for her?"

"Yep."

"Mending fences. Fixing roofs."

"You've got it."

"Then you're in love with Sissy Fox?" she asked with exaggerated innocence.

The springs objected as he sat up. "She's old enough to be my grandma."

"But you've been performing those services for her over the years. Amy told me so." She smiled, pleased with herself at winning a few points, at least.

He was quiet for so long she supposed he was angry and had decided to remain silent. But at last he said,

"There was more between you and me than that, Evvie. More than fixing roofs and mending fences."

"You mean . . ."

"Yes, if you'd have allowed it to happen."

"Would I have been the only woman you'd ever bedded?"

"Now hold on. Whatever you—"

"Were you in love with all those other women?"

He chuckled low in his throat. "You make it sound like a platoon."

"Maybe it was."

"And you sound like a jealous woman."

"Do I?"

"That's no answer." The sound of the springs told her he was getting out of bed. She heard his feet hit the floor and then the barefoot shuffle across the room. He was probably searching for a cigarette he'd overlooked when he'd supposedly kicked the habit. "What do you expect a man to say?" he growled at last. "That you make his heart go pitty-pat?"

How typical of him. Making fun of her. "He's supposed to say what he feels."

She'd forgotten to pull the blinds. The moon looked twice its usual size. Big and white, it had only a sliver missing from its circle. There were two cats outside her window, staring at each other with the concentration only cats can give such a confrontation, deciding if they'll fight.

"There's a giant hole in your carefully worked-out ideas, Evvie," Ryan said.

She swallowed. "What might that be?"

"You claim I asked you to marry me because I made a checklist of wifely qualifications, and you fit."

"In a manner of speaking."

"You have got to be kidding. You're the most mixed-up little wench I've ever known."

"Wench?" She wrinkled her nose at the old-fashioned expression. "Mixed-up how?"

He ignored her question. "Then there's your disposition. You argue constantly."

"An argument requires a minimum of two participants."

"You're a city girl."

"I'm adaptable."

"You're in love with your career."

"I knew that was coming. Just because I—"

"You don't sew. You can't cook worth a damn."

"Now just a darn minute." She sat up, swung her feet to the floor and glared at the wall that separated them.

"The eggs were so overcooked I almost choked on them."

"Both helpings?"

"The bacon was burned."

"Crisp."

"Burned."

"You said it was good."

"I was being polite. Anyway, if I was going over your application for the job as wife, I'd trash it after a single look."

"Who's applying?"

"Take that hogwash of yours about destiny." His springs creaked heavily as he got back into bed again. "A man makes his own destiny."

They were beginning to sound like Jill and Patrick. She got into bed again, too, and smoothed the sheet over her. He said no more and neither did she. It was ten minutes past the hour. Then twenty. She thought about destiny.

Her arrival at the gas station at the same time Ryan was there. What was that but destiny? If he couldn't see it, he was hopeless. And what about Calvin's sending her to Amy to make arrangements for a rehearsal site? The bracelet she had left behind, providing a need for them to see each other again? The wedding? And now, the car that wouldn't start.

The car.

She rolled onto her back and stared at the ceiling. Something Ryan had said suddenly came back to her. He'd once planned to be an auto mechanic. By the time he was fourteen, he could take a car apart and put it back together again. Tonight he'd claimed ignorance.

What about the smudge on his shirt? It was suspiciously like the mark she'd gotten on her arm when she opened the hood of her car. If he'd done any kind of work that would get him dirty, wouldn't he have taken the shirt off first? Unless . . . he'd been in too much of a hurry to do what he wanted to do.

With Calvin it had been flowers sent anonymously over the years, because he was embarrassed about putting his feelings into words. He'd even taken dancing lessons secretly on the side, afraid of looking foolish.

With Ryan, it was the car.

She wasn't going to get poetry out of him, any more than Amy would get it out her new husband. But maybe, if she looked at it a certain way, it *was* a kind of poetry.

She sat up and looked out the window. The two cats were still outside. Neither had changed its position since the last time she'd looked. If one of them didn't make a move, they'd be there all night.

"Ryan, are you asleep?" she called.

He groaned. "I was."

She didn't think so. "I want to talk to you."

"So talk."

"Face-to-face." She reached for her robe. Her pink shorty nightgown left too little to the imagination. "I'm coming in."

"Don't," he warned her, "unless you mean business."

"I do."

In moments she was turning the knob of his door, padding inside, and there they were. He was standing, his shoulders squared and his arms hanging at his sides. He was wearing only the bottoms of a pair of striped pajamas, held up by a narrow cord.

The determination that had bought her this far suddenly evaporated.

"Does Amy have a cat?" she asked, grasping for something to say.

"A what?"

"Two of them are getting ready to fight outside. I thought—"

"Those two are from down the road. It's a game they play, staring each other down every night. Is that what you wanted to talk to me about?"

"I was afraid one of them might get hurt."

"Don't worry."

As the clock struck the half hour, panic turned her knees to jelly. The moment was getting away.

She brushed past him to look out the window. "They're gone."

"Maybe they settled their differences." Coming up behind her, he put his hands on her shoulders. "Good for them."

"Maybe we should do the same thing," she got out at last.

"We have differences?" He feigned surprise.

"One or two."

He lifted her hair and dipped his head to press his lips against the warm skin of her nape.

"None of that now." Resolutely she pulled away and turned to face him. "I'm here to talk."

He grinned an appealing grin that made her feel jointless. "Can't it wait until morning?"

"You want to wait until morning?" she echoed.

"Morning," he repeated, confidence in the moment coloring his voice.

"Before or after you put my car back the way it was before you tinkered with it?"

He lowered his chin to his chest and gave her a sheepish grin. "How did you know?"

She tapped a finger against her forehead. "The question isn't *how* I know—it's *why* you did it."

He shrugged. "To keep you here."

"And why did you want to keep me here?"

He shifted his weight from one foot to the other and groaned. "You're a hard woman, Evelina Pettit."

"Why did you want to keep me here?" she persisted.

"Because . . . because I love you. I guess."

She thought her heart would burst. "Now let's hear it without the 'I guess,'" she said.

He inhaled sharply. "I love you."

"Once more with feeling," she said, coaching him as she had when she was directing his performance as Blackjack Sykes.

"I love you!" he very nearly shouted.

"Very good," she said, her voice breaking despite her attempt to sound firm.

"I love you," he said once again without prompting. "I saw you getting away from me and I was afraid. It's been a long time since I felt so afraid. I had to do something. The car was there. You were still at the church. I couldn't resist it."

"I'm glad you didn't. Resist, I mean." She stepped toward him, backing him against the wall, and tilted her mouth to accept the kiss that was long overdue.

"None of that," he said with new sternness, pretending to push her away. "We're here to talk, remember?"

"We've finished talking."

"Not by a long shot. We'll start by making a few ground rules." He chewed his lower lip. "I go first."

"What kind of ground rules?" she asked, sliding her arms around his neck.

"For starters, you stop hanging evil traits on me. When I took the part of Blackjack, it wasn't typecasting."

She giggled. "Fair enough."

"And..."

"There's an 'and'?"

"There is. Everything about you excites me, Evvie. Your hair, your eyes, your smile and, for the sake of moving on, ditto the rest of your physical attributes. But when it comes down to it, it's the person you are inside that makes me feel the way I do. The way you look is just frosting on the cake."

He sounded so serious. "What you're saying is—"

"What I'm saying is that next time we're in the company of this glamorous sister of yours and she's got her figure back again, allow me do a little leering. I'll be her brother-in-law, and it'll be my privilege."

She bit back a cry of exultation. If he was asking her to marry him again, this time she knew what the answer would be—except that he wasn't asking, he was telling.

"Fair enough," she agreed, unable to think of any words that would express what she was feeling. "Now may I kiss you?"

"That's exactly what I was about to ask you."

It was a kiss filled with tenderness and passion, with unconditional surrender and victory—with memories of the past and previews of the future. A kiss that only two people who'd run headlong into brick walls and toppled them could share.

When it was over, he pulled back to consider her, with one eye closed and his wonderful mustache twitching. "Well?"

"Well what?"

"Don't *you* have to say it?"

She smiled. So in spite of all his talk of practicality, he needed reassurance, too. "You know I love you. That goes without saying."

"Whoa there. According to your own rules, *nothing* goes without saying."

"I was right," she whispered almost to herself.

"About what?"

"About you and me. About our meeting. About our falling in love. It was destiny."

"A man makes his own destiny," he muttered.

"I know," she said, wondering what might have happened if she'd held firm and stayed on her side of the door. She rose on tiptoe to meet the next kiss halfway. "So does a woman."

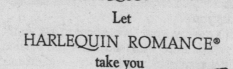

**Fifty red-blooded, white-hot, true-blue hunks
from every State in the Union!**

Look for MEN MADE IN AMERICA! Written by some
of our most poplar authors, these stories feature fifty of
the strongest, sexiest men, each from a different state in
the union!

Two titles available every other month at your favorite
retail outlet.

In March, look for:

TANGLED LIES by Anne Stuart (Hawaii)
ROGUE'S VALLEY by Kathleen Creighton (Idaho)

In May, look for:

LOVE BY PROXY by Diana Palmer (Illinois)
POSSIBLES by Lass Small (Indiana)

You won't be able to resist MEN MADE IN AMERICA!

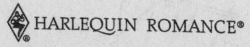

HARLEQUIN ROMANCE®

Question: **What will excite & delight Debbie Macomber's fans?**
Answer: A sequel to her popular 1993 novel,
READY FOR ROMANCE!

Last year you met the two Dryden brothers, Damian and Evan, in
Debbie Macomber's READY FOR ROMANCE. You saw Damian fall in
love with Jessica Kellerman....

Next month watch what happens when Evan discovers that
Mary Jo Summerhill —the love of his life, the woman who'd
rejected him three years before—_isn't_ married, after all!

Watch for READY FOR MARRIAGE: Harlequin Romance #3307
available in April wherever Harlequin books are sold

If you missed READY FOR ROMANCE, here's your chance to order:

#03288   READY FOR ROMANCE   Debbie Macomber $2.99 ☐

(limited quantities available)

TOTAL AMOUNT	$	
POSTAGE & HANDLING	$	
($1.00 for one book, 50¢ for each additional)		
APPLICABLE TAXES*	$ _____	
TOTAL PAYABLE	$ _____	
(Send check or money order—please do not send cash)		

To order, complete this form and send it, along with a check or money order for the
total above, payable to Harlequin Books, to: **In the U.S.:** 3010 Walden Avenue,
P.O. Box 9047, Buffalo, NY 14269-9047; **In Canada:** P.O. Box 613, Fort Erie, Ontario,
L2A 5X3.

Name: _____
Address: _____ City: _____
State/Prov.: _____ Zip/Postal Code: _____

*New York residents remit applicable sales taxes.
 Canadian residents remit applicable GST and provincial taxes.

HRRFM

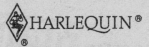

HARLEQUIN®

COMING SOON TO
A STORE NEAR YOU...

THE MAIN
ATTRACTION

By *New York Times* Bestselling Author

This March, look for THE MAIN ATTRACTION by popular
author Jayne Ann Krentz.

Ten years ago, Filomena Cromwell had left her small town
in shame. Now she is back determined to get her sweet,
sweet revenge....

Soon she has her ex-fiancé, who cheated on her with
another woman, chasing her all over town. And he isn't
the only one. Filomena lets Trent Ravinder catch her.

Can she control the fireworks she's set into motion?

Harlequin Romance invites you...

BACK TO THE RANCH

As you enjoy your Harlequin Romance® BACK TO THE RANCH stories each month, you can collect four proofs of purchase to redeem for an attractive gold-toned charm bracelet complete with five Western-themed charms. The bracelet will make a unique addition to your jewelry collection or a distinctive gift for that special someone.

One proof of purchase can be found in the back pages of each BACK TO THE RANCH title...one every month until May 1994.

To receive your gift, please fill out the information below and mail four (4) original proof-of-purchase coupons from any Harlequin Romance **BACK TO THE RANCH** title plus $2.50 for postage and handling (check or money order—do not send cash), payable to Harlequin Books, to: **IN THE U.S.**: P.O. Box 9056, Buffalo, NY, 14269-9056; **IN CANADA**: P.O. Box 621, Fort Erie, Ontario, L2A 5X3.

Requests must be received by June 30, 1994.

Please allow 4-6 weeks after receipt of order for delivery.

BACK TO THE RANCH

NAME: _____
ADDRESS: _____
_____
CITY: _____
STATE/PROVINCE: _____
ZIP/POSTAL CODE: _____
ACCOUNT NO.: _____

ONE PROOF OF PURCHASE   091 KAX